To my favorite aunt & uncle. Thank you for your support. Love you XO Chrissy

For the Love of the Ocean

CHRISTINE LYNN LOURENCO

Copyright © 2015 Christine Lynn Lourenco.

All rights reserved. No part of this book may be used or reproduced by any means, graphic, electronic, or mechanical, including photocopying, recording, taping or by any information storage retrieval system without the written permission of the author except in the case of brief quotations embodied in critical articles and reviews.

Archway Publishing books may be ordered through booksellers or by contacting:

Archway Publishing
1663 Liberty Drive
Bloomington, IN 47403
www.archwaypublishing.com
1 (888) 242-5904

Because of the dynamic nature of the Internet, any web addresses or links contained in this book may have changed since publication and may no longer be valid. The views expressed in this work are solely those of the author and do not necessarily reflect the views of the publisher, and the publisher hereby disclaims any responsibility for them.

Any people depicted in stock imagery provided by Thinkstock are models, and such images are being used for illustrative purposes only. Certain stock imagery © Thinkstock.

ISBN: 978-1-4808-2643-4 (sc)
ISBN: 978-1-4808-2644-1 (e)

Library of Congress Control Number: 2015921232

Print information available on the last page.

Archway Publishing rev. date: 12/28/2015

For the Love of the Ocean

Chapter 1

A Seaside Community

As I sit on the porch of our seaside home on the very swing where my father used to sit listening to the sounds of the ocean, it's hard to believe it's been just about five years since my parents' fatal car crash. The soothing sounds of the waves crashing and the vision of people jogging and biking on the boardwalk this late afternoon didn't help my pain. Neither did the margarita on the rocks with lots of sea salt around the edge of the glass that I held firmly in my hand. I only had the occasional drink but margaritas were my favorite. I am sitting here alone in "our" house; I couldn't help but wonder what life would have been like with them here for my college years. I was only sixteen years old when the accident happened. I went through what should have been exciting milestones in my life alone…getting my driver's license, senior prom, graduating high school and now I would be graduating college in just about a week. I couldn't wait for them to call my name – Summer Wright – I finally made it. It would just be so difficult though to watch everyone with their families celebrating and having huge parties for graduation and I would simply get my diploma and hang it on my empty wall and pat myself on my own back. It was lonely and sad not to have anyone to share it with.

As the wind blew my long blonde hair and made my light blue

sundress sway, I thought of the people that were so important to me in my life. Change was upon me but I knew who I wanted to be by my side every step of the way. I am glad that of course there are people in my life that are celebrating and happy for my achievements but it's just not the same and no one would understand what I mean unless they have lost a parent. I know my parents would be so incredibly proud of me, as they always were though. They would be proud I pursued my dream of marine biology, proud that I didn't party too much or go down the wrong path, or date really bad guys. I hope they can see how I try to keep their memory alive every day. Whether it's buying fresh flowers like my Mom always did, looking at their pictures, sharing stories about them with others, and of course staying involved with the beaches and the community. I wanted them to live on. I sometimes wonder if they can see me somehow…see how I was able to maintain their home, although I never venture out of the upstairs apartment. When I think of them though, most of all, I just miss them terribly.

I hoped to someday create a foundation in my parents' honor. Perhaps it would be something with Monmouth University's marine biology program. It was something I wanted to do eventually. Maybe it would provide scholarship opportunities, updated equipment for the labs, or other things that the students could take advantage of. Or maybe the foundation could provide educational opportunities for younger children to get them interested in marine life and ocean conservation. The oceans cover more than two-thirds of Earth and are full of life. We could teach them about how life thrives in the oceans and learn about the chemical makeup of water, teach them about marine mammals, fish and plants, etc. I wanted to continue my passion for the oceans and the beaches but honor my parents too. I knew my parents would love it, especially my father. He grew up here and loved this town.

I grew up in a seaside town called Avon-by-the-Sea in New Jersey. It's pronounced "Ave-on-by-the-sea". If you say "Ay"von, like the cosmetic company, people will know you are not a local. It was really the best kept secret on the Jersey Shore as the town liked to say. It had beautiful beaches lined with sand dollars. Residents and guests sailed from the marina, spent time shopping and dining at the many up-scale shops and restaurants. It was a great place to fish. You would see fisherman fishing in Sylvan Lake, Shark River and of course in the ocean. It was also a great place to surf. Surfing was something I had been doing since the age of four. I have had wetsuits and surfboards since a toddler. Our house is large and right across the street from the ocean with unobstructed ocean views from every window. It's a beautiful blue color with a wrap-around porch. It has a blue and white striped awning and shutters on the windows. Cool ocean breezes were always here to greet me from one of the 3 open-air decks. We also had a huge year-round sun porch in the back. And, it's spacious with six bedrooms and four and one-half bathrooms. One of the bedrooms has a separate entrance through stairs on the side of the house. I think it was meant to be a maid's quarters. It was more like an apartment than a bedroom, with a small kitchen, large bathroom and living room area too. This is where I was now. Being in the larger part of the house always felt so lonely and just so difficult for me. I can still picture my mother, Carissa, in the kitchen cooking dinner or my father, Edward, on the porch sitting on the swing reading a book. The happy memories are locked away in the main part of the house that I rarely enter. It was like I was afraid to revisit them and I didn't want anyone else to either.

There was a long boardwalk across from us too and I would often ride my bike early in the morning along the boardwalk before it got too crowded. It was such a beautiful place to live. I enjoyed riding my bike and enjoying the fresh air, the sounds of the waves crashing, and watching the seagulls fly over the sand or someone flying a kite. There was a lot of peace in your life when you lived by the beach. I liked to watch the people pass by too. I wondered about their lives and made up scenarios in my head about them. There were two women that went speed walking every morning at 5:00 a.m. I would make up stories in my mind that they were two powerful executives that only had time to exercise at the crack of dawn. There was also this older gentleman that rode an elliptical bicycle every morning. It looked pretty cool. My dad told me it was a pretty grueling workout but at least you got to ride it and see the sights of the ocean instead of using a stationary bike in your house. I envisioned this man as a health nut who worked at an energy drink store and gave lectures on healthy living.

Our house is modern, simple, and comfortable. It has so many relaxing tones of blues and grays and has always felt like a retreat. It is natural and more comfortable than most homes. The highlight is a shell chandelier. It may sound odd or possibly tacky, but it is actually quite beautiful. My mom and I had taken a traditional chandelier and added shells and sea glass to it. It came out so wonderful and it was truly amazing the way the lights reflected off the blue and green tones of the sea glass. It was elegant and a great conversation piece. I remember making it with my mom when I was young. Of course, she did most of it, but at the time I felt like I worked really hard on it. My mom always treasured that chandelier and it was something we had done together so I knew I would always have that light no matter what house I ended up in some day. Every shell and piece of sea glass on that chandelier was found by me or my mom. My mom and I always did projects together.

Cooking was another thing my mother always did, and she taught me a lot around the kitchen. She loved to make flavorful sauces and use unexpected spices to make food truly amazing. She would use lots of papaya and mango in seafood dishes or she would season meats with her own rubs that she created like my personal favorite rub of sea salt, black pepper, dried onion, garlic salt and green tea. That green tea just gave it that extra special taste. Cooking was something I learned from her well and it had become an escape of some form for me. I enjoyed trying new recipes or coming up with my own. In fact, just the night before, my closest friend Chase had come over to enjoy my latest creation. It was a shrimp and scallop dish. I sautéed garlic, fresh basil, edamame, white wine, salt, black pepper and onion and then added in the shrimp and scallops. I served it over bow tie pasta with grape tomatoes and a light cream sauce. It was absolutely delicious. Cooking wasn't something people would expect from a girl in her twenties. But, I knew guys liked that I could cook. They all secretly want their mothers to still take care of them and I guess there is something maternal about me cooking for them. I looked forward to the day I could cook meals for my family when I get married and have children. I knew I would cherish that time because it was something I haven't had in so long with my parents gone. My mom always took pride in serving healthy and interesting meals for me and my dad. Her family was her life and she took good care of me.

My father was a surgeon and came from money to begin with so we always had it really good. We traveled a lot and always had the best of everything. We were the three musketeers, as my mom always said. My mom was a gorgeous woman. She had the same long, blonde hair that I did and I was happy to have her blue eyes that matched the ocean. Every time I look in the mirror, I see her. Both my parents had a strong love for the ocean and the beach, which is probably where I get it from. Actually, it's definitely where I get it from. Between me and my mom, we must have collected thousands of sea shells. Growing up we would be out there for hours combing the beaches especially in the off-season. The beaches were empty during off-season and shells would line the beaches for miles. I would color and decorate them, make them into art projects like jewelry or glue them onto things, but the special ones I would save. I have the most prized ones in my bedroom. I still look at them in awe all the time. There's just something so fascinating and astonishing about them. Growing up, I used to label jars with the names of different types of shells and as I found them throughout the summer or on vacations, I would then bring them home and put them in the jar they belonged in. I had a jar for sea glass colors too – blue, clear, green, purple, and so on. Anyone who knows me well can see that I am pretty obsessed with shells. I had every book on sea shells too to learn more about them.

We grew up surfing too and I still do it almost every chance I can.

My friends and I often entered local surf competitions and I have the trophies in my bedroom to prove it. Surfing was a big part of living at the beach in this town. I have had so many wet suits and rash guards in my life that they could fill up a closet. In fact I just bought a new wet suit and got a new custom board with pink & yellow stripes down the sides. I couldn't wait to get on that new board. On weekends, my parents and I would go out and ride the waves before breakfast. I remember hanging ten on my pretty pink board. It was such a charmed life. I don't think they could've picked any other name for me than the name they chose – Summer. It just fits. Growing up, my mom stayed home and didn't work full-time so she was always there for me. We were definitely like best friends. She was always driving me somewhere…to gymnastics, cheerleading, and the aquarium. Our visits to the aquarium and spending so much time on the beach is how I knew from a young age, I would work with marine life in some way. I was always the kid at the beach digging for crabs, finding shark teeth and sand dollars, catching starfish and jelly fish too. I just loved it. It was really always the simple things like collecting shells or going for a ride on the boardwalk on our bikes that I remember and enjoyed the most of all the times with my parents….the simple things in life….not the money, the material stuff or the vacations.

My family did a lot for the community too. My dad spent a lot of time cleaning up the beaches and holding fundraisers to take care of our beaches and community. Yes, the Wright Family was a pretty important part of this town. Conservation of the ocean and the protection and restoration of marine species and ecosystems to restore populations and habitats were so important to my parents. My dad worked hard to try and mitigate people and their harmful activities like pollution, littering, overfishing and more. All of these things affect the beaches, the ocean and the marine life and we would no longer have these things to enjoy if people who cared didn't fight for them to protect the environment. My dad had grown up in Avon-by-the-Sea and had vowed to protect this seaside town and its natural beauty and charm. When my dad went away to college, he met my mom and they fell in love. They vowed to come back and raise a family in Avon-by-the-Sea, which they did. People asked my parents why they loved it here so much and my dad would always have the same answer – "for the love of the ocean". He meant it too…I have never seen anyone care so much about this town and its beaches. My parents said living here was a dream come true – the best of all worlds. Feeling like you are away on vacation all the time and a part of a terrific, close-knit community described this town. I didn't realize at the time how much I would need that close-knit community's support one day.

About five houses down directly on the ocean is the Minella family. Their house is ten times larger in size and in price because the ocean is in their backyard. It made my million-dollar home seem like a bungalow. And, it's a beautiful home indeed….make that a gorgeous home. It's a brown huge house with tons of windows. It has a whopping eight bedrooms and eight and a half bathrooms. It was easily worth over $6 million dollars. It really is an architectural masterpiece with a panoramic ocean-view and of course, a direct ocean access. The inside was even nicer than the outside. Plain and simple, it's exquisite. It has a custom interior with glass walkways, radiant heated floors, and a state of the art kitchen that should be featured on HGTV, bedrooms with private baths, an exercise room, a 4-car garage, a media room and more. I loved spending time in their beautiful home. Abbie Minella's grandfather had owned a huge hotel chain and she had inherited a lot of money and she loved to invest in real estate. This house was no exception and it was their primary home and indeed the most beautiful home in all of Avon-by-the-Sea.

Sam and Abbie Minella have two sons, Chase and Ryan. Chase is the exact same age as me, but a few months older and he just turned twenty-two years old. Chase has dirty blonde hair and hazel green eyes and abs to die for. He is tall and handsome. Ryan is nineteen now and also very handsome. Ryan's hair is light brown and he is about two inches shorter than Chase. We all grew up together and considered each other family. That was easy to do since my father and Sam Minella grew up together and even went to medical school together. They had known each other their whole life. They both wanted to move back to this seaside town and stuck to it. They were also both doctors at Monmouth Hospital. Abbie didn't work either like my Mom. Abbie didn't financially need too. And, handling Chase and Ryan was definitely enough to keep her hands full. Chase and Ryan surfed pretty much every day and they were handsome, fun and active. Between football, soccer, basketball and baseball on top of surfing, Abbie was a busy woman. She could afford the best nannies in the world if she wanted to but that wasn't her style. She was very hands on and Abbie and my mom were very close friends.

Every summer break (and all year long really) was the ultimate time for our two families. We would be on the beach all day and have huge barbecues and parties at night together. We vacationed together, ate dinners out together, hung out at each other's houses, got box seats at NY Giants Football games or went to concerts together. We were all inseparable. Especially Chase and I…we are best friends. I couldn't imagine my life without him. Yes, he tortured me a lot too growing up, but I love him and his family to death. I wouldn't be able to survive without them. Every summer, Chase and I would go to a marine life camp at the local aquarium. He was also in football camp too at the end of the summer and I did cheerleading. Ryan wanted nothing to do with any camps. He was such a mama's boy when he was younger, whether he would admit it or not. The marine life camp though was a favorite of Chase and mine. There was just something magical about that place and it was just an extension of the beach in a way and we just loved it. It was where Chase and I were truly educated on the aspects of marine life and conservation. Chase always loved the shark exhibit and I loved the penguins.

Aside from the Minella family, there were others in my inner circle too. There's Chase's buddy Mercer. Mercer is a total surfer dude. His straggly red hair and board shorts are how I envision him always. I don't think he has ever owned any clothes that didn't belong to a surfer-branded company. But that is Mercer; he wouldn't be Mercer without those qualities. He definitely fit that image. And, he is a gem and a great friend to me too. Mercer was a lifeguard growing up on the beach and spent all his free time surfing or working part-time at the surf shop in town too. I owe all of my discount purchases at that place to him. He is a chick-magnet because let's face it, girls love lifeguards and surfers and the fact that he did both, he is like a God. Mercer and Chase together spells T-R-O-U-B-L-E. And behind that trouble is a line of girls wanting their attention. Despite Mercer's bad boy image, he was a sweetheart. I knew he would always have my best interests in mind. Like Chase, I know I could call Mercer at 3:00 a.m. and he would come for me. He is definitely a really good friend. Mercer's parents live about two blocks down in a huge house also on the beach. His dad works on Wall Street in New York City and takes the ferry in every day. His mom is an artist and has a local gallery in town to sell her work. Adelaide's Artwork is the name of her trendy store. She is a talented woman in her own right and does quite well for herself. I think he gets his easy-going ways from his mom.

Mel, short for Melanie, is my best friend since 2nd grade when she moved here. Unlike Chase, Mercer and me, she came from nothing. Her parents, John and Leticia, owned a small apartment above their donut shop in town and are still there after all these years. Best donuts I have ever had though and we still went there every Sunday morning for breakfast after a late night out. They have a small closet at this donut shop though that we called the boogie man's home growing up. It is like a sound-proof little closet. One time Mel's dad had gotten locked in there and no one could find him for hours. He was knocking but you couldn't hear him. I still don't know why they didn't just remove that door for safety purposes. Their donut shop is a main attraction in town. On weekends, everyone is there and in the summer, it is very busy all the time. Mel helped them out on days that she didn't have school or during busy rushes when they needed her. Her heart though, like mine, is in marine biology so she works often at the aquarium in town with me. As soon as college started, we had worked part-time there to gain experience and full-time in the summer to help with the camp program. Mainly, Mel just sleeps over my house and is like my live-in roommate anyway. We are like sisters. We are attending the university, working together, and hanging out at the clubs and beach on weekends so she stays often and keeps me company.

Mel is dating Ronnie. Ronnie goes to school with us too, but he grew up in Middletown, NJ not too far from us. He is tall and thin and told me that in high school if there was a category for "best nerd" that would have been him. He is a science nerd at heart but he wasn't nerdy in the looks department. He is tall and has dark skin and dark, black hair. He is a mix of Cuban and Chinese. There is something almost exotic looking about him and Mel sure noticed that. He is a great guy and good to Mel. I knew when I first met Ronnie that he was in love with Mel. It was hard not to be…Mel is so beautiful. She has wavy, dark hair and her brown eyes are stunning but her skin is what the most amazing thing is. I don't think she has ever had a blemish. I don't know if it's her half white/half black ethnicity or some secret skin cream, but Mel will probably never need to wear make-up in her life. Mel is super tall too. She has long, lean legs. She was always self-conscious of her height growing up but I always envied it. I am only 5 feet 3 inches and tiny. I could eat 2 Big Macs from McDonalds and never gain a pound. I think I am eternally 94 lbs. Mel said she envied me for being so small and thin. I guess you always want what you don't have. I always wanted her long, lean legs. Mel, Ronnie, Chase, Mercer and I had just finished up our final semester at Monmouth University and we would all graduate soon. We were getting through or done with the last of finals. Things seem to be progressing nicely from that front.

Then there's Amy. It was her last semester at the university too and she had gone to our high school so I have known her a long time. She is also known as "Psycho Amy" as Chase called her. Amy is short with brown hair down to her shoulders. She never seemed to like me and I thought she was kind of snobby. She is actually kind of cute and nice but she always liked Chase a little too much and that made him uncomfortable. Chase made the mistake of hooking up with her a few times during drunken nights. Now, she is stalking him. I wasn't sure if Chase liked the attention or if it aggravated him or a little of both. Chase was definitely known as a player. Girls would always come to me asking for advice on how to figure him out but the truth is I couldn't help them. I was still trying to do that myself… I was always picking up the pieces for Chase. There was more than one occasion that he had come knocking on my door at 2:00 a.m. saying he texted his parents that he was staying at my house or Mercer's house so that he didn't have to go home. There were a few times that he had one of his latest girls with him and they wanted to "use" my couch if you know what I mean. Other times, he was just drunk and wanted me to nurse him back to health. I was always making him coffee, cooking him breakfast, or cleaning up his vomit. Boy did he owe me big time!

Last but not least is our next door neighbor Stella. She is just so unexpected, witty and amorous. She has grey hair that is always in a bun. I don't think I have ever seen her wear it down. She always has a smock on because she loves to paint. I think she does it every day non-stop. She is quirky and crazy, artsy and sweet and absolutely loves animals, especially dogs. She has four dogs. She used to have cats too but I am allergic so when her cat passed away she never got another one. I knew she did it for me. She is my buddy. She taught me a lot. Her husband had died about eight years ago and her only son, Brice, lived across the country in California. He works in the movie business. I think she saw me as her child too in some strange way. She always babysat for me growing up and knew the Minella Family really well too. Like I mentioned, she painted a lot and spent a lot of time painting the ocean, the beach and the people of the community. She has a great one that she did of me and Chase surfing. I didn't even know she had done it until I was over there one day and saw it. She never really told anyone about her art. You just sort of discovered it on your own. She was also friendly with Mercer's mom since they had art in common. But unlike Mercer's mom, Stella never sold any of her work. She said she did it for herself and the love of it.

Her other love was definitely dogs. Stella just loves her dogs and they are like her children. Her dogs are all different sizes and it is quite comical to see her try and walk them. The off-season is the best because she could just let them run on the beach and there is never really anyone around. Her dogs are her family. One is a German short-haired pointer named Ben. She also has a bull dog named Barry, a poodle named Buck (you see the "b" and boy name pattern here) and finally (my favorite) a little guy named Bobby who is a Yorkshire terrier. Yorkies are my favorite type of dog in the whole world. I had wanted one since forever. We had one growing up named "Buttercup" but after he died, my mom was too heart-broken to get another one. I definitely wanted another one someday. I pretended Bobby was mine anyway. He came on bike rides with Chase and me and rode in my basket. He is just too adorable for words. I would sneak him into stores and restaurants. No one ever knew he was even with me; he is always so quiet and good. Chase loves dogs too. I would always see him stopping by Stella's house to see her dogs and Chase and I took turns taking care of them whenever Stella traveled across the country to see her son. Stella may be a neighbor but she was like a second mom to me and luckily I have her in my life. I would need her motherly ways more than I ever thought.

Chapter 2

Cruising into Margaritaville

This is where it all began….how I ended up here sitting on my father's swing on my porch; alone.

Spring Break and sixteen years old were a good combination in my opinion. This year, we would be going with the Minella Family on a cruise to the Bahamas and some other islands. Chase and I could not wait! We would fly down to Florida and leave from the port there. We would be going to the Bahamas, St. Maarten and St. Thomas including a few days out at sea cruising. I couldn't wait to get a head start on my tan for the summer and it was going to be another fun time with our two families. We had vacationed together all over the world – Hawaii, Canada, Portugal, England, Spain and a lot of islands in the Caribbean. We hadn't done a cruise yet though so we were all excited. I had heard that you gain ten pounds on a cruise there is so much food. Chase had heard that open seas means no drinking age so of course he was ready to take advantage of that. My parents couldn't wait to see the sites of the islands and take advantage of seeing the many shows they had on board.

We flew down to Florida early on Saturday morning in order to make the 1:00 p.m. cruise time. We made it in plenty of time although Chase took forever to come out when the car service picked us up to take us to the airport. I swear he took more time than a girl to get ready. He uses more hair products than me. I go with the natural look and mainly wear my long hair down, in braids, or in a ponytail. Simple was really more of my thing. Chase always looked and dressed to impress. "It's all for the ladies" he would always say but I think he did it because he liked it. We made it finally to the cruise ship and boarded after showing our documentation. Our suitcases were being dropped off at our rooms so that we could go on deck and wave to the people watching the ship pull out into the open sea. The cruise ship pulled away and everyone's families seeing them off and bystanders waved goodbye. We made it into our rooms and started to unpack our stuff and get the rooms in order to be comfortable for the week. We had three rooms in total, all in a row. Our parents had their own rooms and we had a "kid" room, although we were hardly "kids" anymore. I think our parents still viewed us as little kids or maybe they just trusted us enough to have our own space.

The rooms were small but comfortable and we had a balcony off of each room. We had to go to a safety session on the deck to learn about boat safety before anyone was really allowed to do anything. We learned how to put on life vests and where the life boats were located. It made me briefly think of the Titanic and I was glad we were in warm, tropical water and not icy cold water. As we walked back to our room from the session, Chase reiterated that he was exceptionally excited for the cruise because they really didn't check your I.D. on the ship and he wanted to get 'toasty' as he called it. I barely drank so he couldn't wait to get me drunk and see what I would be like. More torture from him as always. I was just looking forward to having fun and getting a tan. The first day was almost over by the time we flew down to FL, set sail and got into our rooms. It was already dinner time and each night at dinner was a different theme. Tonight though was just a welcome type of casual dinner. There was so much food that I think I already gained 5 pounds after one dinner! They had a lot of amazing ice sculptures and creative food displays too. They really went all out and you could tell this was going to be a first-class experience. The ship had a night club on board too and Chase, Ryan and I would be checking it out as soon as dinner was done.

"I want you boys to behave and not torture Summer" said Abbie.
"Summer is the one you need to worry about" joked Chase.
"Somehow I find that hard to believe" replied Abbie.

Our parents were going to some show they had on board. Some lame singing and dancing show as Chase put it. We didn't care as long as we had free reign to roam around the boat. We went to the bar by the pool first and of course, Chase already had many friends on the boat. I didn't know how he did it. We had only been on the boat for a few hours and he knew everyone. Chase was smart too and made sure he befriended some guys that were twenty-one, the legal drinking age, just in case. Chase and a few of his new found friends came over and we got a table near the bar and they brought lots of drinks. Chase gave me a margarita. It was the first time I had ever had one and I absolutely LOVED it. It was on the rocks, sea salt on the rim and oh so good! It went down really easily and I was on to the next. I never drank. First of all, I am underage and I just have never really had the desire. Sure, I was curious to try some things but I liked to be in control and know what I am doing. Being a small person too, I knew my tolerance would be really low and I never wanted to risk being taken advantage of. At least I had Chase here to protect me but with my parents here too, I had to be careful.

We hit the night club next. There was a whole group of us now and I didn't even know anyone's name. Ryan said he was tired and headed back to the room. I think he was just a little younger and nervous about being around a group of party people drinking. Chase put his arm around me and we headed into the club. My cheeks were red and I had a permanent smile on my face. I guess the alcohol was starting to sink in....

"You are so toasty right now", laughed Chase, *"I love it"*.

> "Shut up! I am not drinking anymore because if our parents find out, this cruise will become a lot more boring when we are locked in our rooms" I told Chase.

We all danced well into the night. It was about 12:30 a.m. We headed out and hugged our new friends as if we'd known them forever. We had such a good time. If this was just the beginning of this trip, I couldn't imagine what the rest would have in store for us. It was definitely off to a more than perfect start. We headed up to our room and I saw my dad in the hallway entering his room. I could tell he was just pretending and was probably really waiting up to see that we got in o.k. and not too late.

> "You are taking care of my girl, Chase?" said my dad.
> "I promise to always take care of Summer" said Chase.
> "Good night Daddy. Love you."

I kissed my dad on the cheek and Chase and I entered the room where Ryan was fast asleep. I brushed my teeth with Chase and he kept pushing me so that I couldn't see myself in the mirror. He was always a joker and torturing me. Chase gave me a kiss on the cheek and we went to sleep. I remember passing out as soon as I hit the pillow. I was exhausted and I wasn't used to drinking so the room was spinning a little. Thank God I had stopped drinking when I did, I thought.

The next day when we woke up we were in the Bahamas. We ate breakfast and watched as the cruise ship pulled into the port at Nassau.

> "It's better in the Bahamas" joked Ryan.
> "What is the plan for today?" I asked.
> "We are going to walk around the straw market and then after lunch do some snorkeling" said my mom.
> "Yes!" said Chase and I simultaneously.

We both loved the marine life and couldn't wait to see it close up. My mom, Abbie and I headed out to do some shopping at the straw market. I couldn't get over all the stands and things that they had. They had some amazing and unique items. Everywhere I went islanders wanted to braid my long hair. I finally broke down and let them do one braid. I didn't want a million braids like I saw a lot of people get done. I was too conservative for that and didn't really let anyone except myself and my mom mess with my hair. We left the straw market and headed into town to the more traditional stores too. Abbie bought me some perfume and a Gucci purse at one of the stores in town. She was always buying me gifts. My mom, Abbie and I had a great morning. The boys stayed on the ship and went to the gym and hung out swimming. They couldn't be bothered with shopping. We joined them back on the ship for lunch and then headed out to snorkel. A tour bus picked us up and we were on our way. We arrived at a beautiful beach, not that all the beaches weren't amazing here. The water was crystal blue and clear as glass. Palm trees lined the edges of the beach and there were locals and vacationers enjoying the beautiful day. The sand almost looked like it had hints of pink like I had seen in Bermuda and I could only imagine the shells I would find. We were forced to sit through an educational training and then were finally able to head out into the water. To my dismay, they didn't let you take any shells, fruits or other types of items from the island onto the ship for fear of passing infections or other things. As we walked towards the water, one of the tour guides gave us some corn on the cobs to bring out into the waters and feed the fish. He said it was only for those who could "handle it" since the fish will gather completely around you. Ryan acted like he didn't hear and didn't take any. I definitely took one and of course, Chase, always trying to out-do me, took two.

Our parents were hanging out at the bar there having drinks. They didn't even go out to snorkel yet. I think they really just signed up for this because they knew Chase and I would want to go really badly. Ryan, Chase and I headed out into the water.

"Don't come near me with that corn" said Ryan.
"You are such a baby, Ryan" teased Chase.
*"Leave him alone Chase. We'll stay at least one hundred
yards away from you, Ryan"* I told him.

Ryan floated off but remained within sight as we all had our heads in the water looking at all the fish swimming by. There were schools of colorful fish. There was a reef below us so we were really careful and it was none short of amazing. I knew I would always cherish this experience. We looked down at the life below us. It was all so mysterious and astounding to watch. Chase and I swam below the surface and held out our corn as the fish came up and surrounded us gnawing away at it. The fish swam all around us and I looked at Chase and he smiled. He mouthed "this is unbelievable". We came up for air and just stuck our face in the water to breath out of the tube while Chase held out his second piece of corn. Chase held my hand with his other hand and we watched as fish of all colors…yellow, blue, gray and almost every color of the rainbow gnawed at the corn until it was gone.

"What a cool experience!" said Chase. *"That was incredible".*
"I know." "I can't believe how hungry they are too!" I laughed.
"I'll always remember this. It was awesome!" said Chase.
"Me too" I smiled.
"Not this" said Chase referring to snorkeling *"this"*
he said and pushed my head under water.
*I came up coughing and he just laughed at me
and I couldn't help but laugh too.*
*"I'll especially remember you in your bikini. For a tiny girl, you
fill it out well"* replied Chase and I playfully smacked him.

We caught up with Ryan and teased him about missing out on feeding the corn to the fish. We floated around for another hour or so and then headed back in. The tour bus would be leaving soon and we needed to get back to the ship for dinner. We didn't plan on doing much tonight. All of us were sunburn and tired so we all just hung out and played cards in my parent's room until we called it a night. The next two days would be spent out to sea so we would have plenty of time to party on the ship until we made it to St. Maarten and then St. Thomas before heading back to Florida. Besides my back was really sunburn too. I didn't realize being in the water so long and floating on your stomach watching the fish, my back was facing the sun the entire time.

The next day on the trip was mainly spent at the pool. After breakfast, we went swimming, sat in the hot tub and shared stories from other vacations with the seven us. Later, we ate lunch and enjoyed a gigantic ice cream sundae from their awesome ice cream bar poolside. They literally had every flavor ice cream including some local island flavors. My favorite local flavor was soursop. I had never heard of it before but it tasted like pineapples and strawberries mixed together. I loaded it with sprinkles, chocolate syrup and whipped cream. I skipped the maraschino cherry as those were never really a favorite of mine. My back had definitely had enough sun so we finally left and went back to our rooms to get ready for dinner. After showering, we headed to dinner and then Chase and I could hit the nightclub again while our parents attended another one of their shows. Ryan was going with them this time too so it would be just the two of us. We secretly liked it that way. Chase had texted me at dinner even though we were sitting across from each other saying "Margaritas tonight??" I just gave him a sly grin and thought he just wants me to get drunk. We had an amazing seafood dinner although I told my mom her seafood creations were much better and she winked at me. It was a "dress up" night at dinner as one of their varying themes. I wore a black off-the-shoulder dress that hugged my body and black sandals with a heel. I wore my hair down but curled it to make it wavy. Chase told me I looked "smoking hot". I guess that's a good thing coming from Mr. Man in the Mirror. He looked good too. He had on a grey jacket with a casual shirt under it. In my opinion, he looked 'smoking hot' too but I wasn't going to tell him that. I was way too embarrassed.

We said goodbye to our parents as they headed out to the show and made our way to the night club. Chase and I met up with some British guys that he met snorkeling… yes – he met MORE people even while we were snorkeling. We ordered rounds and rounds of drinks and I can't even remember how many drinks I had. They were small in size so I remember thinking I could handle drinking several of these. Boy was I wrong. We were all dancing and I was definitely wasted. This was probably the first time I was really drunk. One of the British guys was named Chad. It just sounded like such a British name to me probably because I was drunk. I kept saying it over and over and I would make him say my name over and over too because I liked the way it sounded with his adorable accent. I don't even remember what he really looked like because I was too drunk to care and just hung out with him.

"You are wasted!" said Chase. "No, I am not…
o.k." I said laughing "yes, I am" I said
as I hugged Chase and kissed him on the lips and told him I loved him.
"Wow, you really are drunk!" said Chase surprised but happy.
Chad came over and said "Summer, come on over by me".
"No, that's alright Chad, I got her." Chase replied.
"She is fine Chase. We are just hanging out over here on the couches
taking a break from dancing" Chad said grabbing my
hand and pulling me over by the couches.

I remember looking back and Chase looked angry. I couldn't get over the look on his face. I figured he must just be worried about me being so drunk. Chad brought me over to the couch alright and placed me right on top of his lap. I could see Chase over at the bar chatting it up with one of the girls that had been flirting with him since we arrived. I suddenly didn't feel that great. It really irked me for some reason that Chase was always flirting too. Whenever I closed my eyes, the room would spin and I felt really dizzy. I knew I had to get out of there. I told Chad I had to go the bathroom, snuck past Chase and I left. I wasn't sure if it was the alcohol or something with Chase. I just knew I had drank way too much. I made it to the room and thankfully Ryan was asleep and my parents were nowhere in sight. I threw up a couple of times in the toilet and the room was spinning. No wonder I don't really want to drink. This sucks. I felt horrible although I definitely felt a lot better after throwing up. I managed to wash my face and brush my teeth and then pass out into my bed. I passed out cold too because I didn't remember anything from that point on until I got woken up the next morning.

I never did hear Chase come in the night before. Ryan woke me up and Chase wasn't there. He told Chase had gone to the gym and was skipping breakfast. I hoped that Chase wasn't mad at me. I guess I wasn't a very fun drunk after all like he thought I would be. We went to breakfast and I had to pretend I felt o.k. I managed to eat some plain toast and coffee. I was trying not to gag as my parents ate their omelets. The smell of the eggs and orange juice was making me sick. Today was another day at sea too. I just wanted to go back to bed. We left breakfast and went to go get our bathing suits on to hang out again at the pool. I put on my red bikini and threw on a cover-up and grabbed a book I had brought with me. We went up to the pool and got some chairs. There was still no sign of Chase. My parents and I went for a swim and I was feeling a lot better than I was before. I went back up onto my lounge chair and started to read keeping one eye on the book and another out for Chase. I texted him real quick too and said "where are you" but he didn't respond.

Chase finally surfaced and I saw him talking with the group of British friends including the girl I had last seen him talking to. She gave him a kiss on the cheek and then he headed over towards us. After talking with his parents, he came over and sat at the end of my lounge chair.

"Have fun last night?" he said.
"Barely. I definitely drank too many margaritas and went back to the room early and got sick" I said.

*"Really? I thought you left with Chad." said Chase sarcastically.
"Of course not. I barely know him. Why would I
leave with him? I wasn't that drunk!"
I snapped back at him. "Besides, I am not the
one who seems to be hooking up
left and right" I said while glancing over at his British conquest
who he obviously hooked up with.*

Ryan came over and told us to stop fighting. Chase told him we weren't fighting and Ryan and Chase dove into the pool. Chase hated conflict so he did typical Chase and ignored it. I got up to go get a bottle of water because I was still really dehydrated from drinking and as I walked by the pool Chase grabbed my ankle and knocked me in the water. I guess our fight was over. I don't know what we were even fighting about anyway.

We didn't go to the night club that night. We had another themed dinner and it was a late time slot so we just all headed back to the rooms and called it an early night. I was still hung over anyway and didn't think I could take drinking again. My body was definitely trying to rehydrate itself. We had one more day at sea and then the next day we would be stopping in St. Maarten. I had heard so many wonderful things about this island and couldn't wait. We were going to a do some sight-seeing on the island. I was really excited too because we were planning on touring downtown Philipsburg. Our parents were also going to do some gambling on the island and while they were there the three of us "kids" were going horse-back riding on the beach and then meeting back up with them.

We got up early and headed out to go shopping and tour the Philipsburg area. It was a cute, older town and was the capital of the Dutch side of the island. We shopped, ate at a café, shopped again on Front Street and then stopped for some traditional island food for lunch. My parents tried their local drink called 'Ti Punch' and it was lime, rum and sugar cane I think. It looked delicious but I am sure it was named after the punch it gave you of alcohol. Our parents then split off from us to go gamble while they sent us on another "tour". We hopped on the tour bus near the cruise ship and were headed to go horse-back ride on the beach. We would be going on a 2-hour ride along the popular Orient Beach on the French side of the island which was a lot more low-key that the Dutch side. I couldn't wait. When we arrived I thought of Stella and how she would have so much to paint if she were here with us. The sand was almost a velvety white in color and the water a turquoise blue. It really looked like a post-card. We were now on the French side of the island and it was truly spectacular. The beach was packed with people parasailing, drinking, swimming and hanging out. We hopped on our horses and toured the beach and surrounding areas. I found myself slightly embarrassed as Chase watched all the naked sunbathers around as well. Chase could tell.

"You look better naked Summer. Don't worry" laughed Chase.
"Shut up. You have never seen me naked" I told him.
"That's what you think" Chase said coyly.

I really loved St. Maarten and its charm. It was such a unique and intriguing island. I only wish we could've spent more time there. It would be St. Thomas tomorrow and I had heard how gorgeous that island is. We went to dinner as a group again when we returned to the ship. Chase had made plans to hang out in one of the British guy's rooms and didn't seem to really ask me so I just stayed in and hung out with Ryan and read my book. I wondered why Chase didn't ask me. Did he not want me to drink? Or, did he want to hook up with that British girl?

Chase actually went to Chad's room and hung out playing cards and drinking with that crew. He didn't want Summer around them. He didn't want something to happen between her and Chad. The British girl's name was Samantha and she pulled Chase aside and asked him if everything was o.k. I guess it was written all over his face that he was frustrated in some way.

"What's going on with you Chase?" inquired Samantha.
"It's nothing. Just got some stuff on my mind" Chase told her.
"Is it that girl you are with, Summer?" asked Samantha.
"What would make you think that?" asked Chase taken aback.
"I have a sixth sense about this kind of stuff and I
can tell you have strong feelings for her.
Am I right?" inquired Samantha.
"Yes" Chase told her figuring he would never
see her again after this cruise anyway.
"Don't let her slip through your fingers then
and tell her" advised Samantha.
"I have the same feelings for Chad" Samantha shared.
"I am finally going to do something about it.
You should take my advice and do the same. You are obviously in love with Summer" said Samantha. Chase couldn't help but think of Summer in her red bikini. She was so beautiful and sexy in every way. And, he knew her inside and out. She was the perfect girl but he couldn't ever screw it up.
"Thanks Samantha" said Chase kind of
relieved that Chad was sort of taken.

Ryan had fallen asleep and I decided to sneak out and go for a walk. My parents and the Minellas were all asleep. It was 12:30 a.m. and Chase of course was still out. My parents thought I was in for the night so I figured my dad wouldn't be waiting in the hallway looking for me. I walked up by the pool and lay on the lounge chair and looked up at the stars and listened to the ship cruising through the seas. I wondered where Chase was and what he was doing. I felt a little pissed off that he left me out from his latest escapades and acted weird all day. I looked a few chairs down and noticed two people making out. Oh my God, it was Chad and that girl that Chase had hooked up with - Samantha! I wondered if Chase was pissed. Or, maybe he didn't hook up with her at all and just "led" me to believe it. I slowly and quietly got up from my lounge chair and tiptoed so they wouldn't see me. I don't think they would anyway because they were intensely making out. I snuck away so Chad wouldn't see me and decided to just head back to the room. I quietly slid the door to the room open and tiptoed in. I looked over and Ryan was still fast asleep. I looked over at Chase's bed. Chase still wasn't back.

I lay my head on the pillow and couldn't sleep. I was a little sad that Chase had left me out. These trips that our families took together were times I cherished with Chase. We had already had so many great times and I felt like ever since I got drunk, he was mad at me. I never really wanted to drink again if it was going to affect our friendship. Although, it didn't seem fair that Chase could drink, hook up and do whatever he wanted. At 1:30 a.m., Chase finally entered the room. I pretended I was sleeping but I wasn't. I was like my father a few days before, waiting up for him. I could smell the alcohol on him as soon as he walked in the room and couldn't help but wonder if my dad had smelled it on me that night too when I kissed him on the cheek. Chase came over by me and leaned in over me. I could feel his breath on my face. I didn't know what he was doing. Maybe he was checking to see if I was sleeping. He lingered a moment and then went over to his bed. He didn't even brush his teeth or change and just crashed onto his bed fast asleep.

At 7:30 a.m., my parents and the Minella's knocked on our door and Ryan let them in...

"Breakfast and then St. Thomas. We are already docked in the port" said my dad.

We threw on our bathing suits and got ready and all headed down to breakfast. Chase put his arm around me as we walked down. He didn't share anything about what he had done the night before. Typical Chase. After breakfast, we headed out onto the island. It was greener than I thought it would be. We walked through Charlotte Amalie, the capital of the United States Virgin Islands and one of the most popular cruise ports in the Caribbean. Abbie and Sam were checking out some real estate on the island. My parents and I along with Chase and Ryan were left to explore for the day. We decided to rent a Jeep and drove through what almost felt like a French countryside. We saw colorful shops and restaurants and took amazing pictures. I couldn't help but think what a great time all of us had with my parents that day. As much as we liked to lose our parents and do our own thing, it was a wonderful day. Chase and Ryan were laughing with my parents about another vacation we had gone on where we rented a Jeep. I had gotten really car sick for some reason and kept making them stop so I could throw up. I think it was the road to Hana in Hawaii. Chase and Ryan were always picking on me.

We headed back to the cruise ship late. We had stayed on the island as long as possible and skipped the dinner on the cruise ship and met up with Abbie and Sam and ate in Charlotte Amalie while Abbie and Sam talked about investing in property here. I wouldn't mind that. I would love to come back here. It truly was a beautiful place to visit or even live. We were at the restaurant for hours eating, drinking and laughing. Abbie loved St. Thomas and had been there many times so she knew the island really well. She told us stories of going here when she was a child. Before you knew it, it was late. The ship was leaving at around 11:30 p.m. and we literally walked back on the ship at a few minutes past 11:00 p.m. We were all exhausted and called it a night. Tomorrow was our last day at sea until we headed back to Florida and then we would fly back to New Jersey to go home.

The next day we were up early to make the most of our final day and just grabbed some breakfast by the pool. We had been lucky with the weather and it was another gorgeous day. The seas were pretty calm too. I had heard horror stories of people getting really sick from rough seas and I was glad we had gone before hurricane season. Mel's parents went on a Disney Cruise right after a hurricane had passed. They said the boat was rocking the entire time and people were so sick that you had to walk around vomit in every hallway and they gave them straps to hook themselves into bed so they wouldn't fall out. They said dinners were empty because people were so sick they couldn't leave their rooms. I remember they said they were supposed to go to a private island for a barbecue and swim and the island was destroyed in the hurricane too and they couldn't even enjoy that part of the trip either. Luckily, we didn't have that happen to us. I tried to ignore that it was almost over because I really didn't want to go back to school on Monday. Ryan, Chase and I hung out by the pool going down all the slides and playing cards on the lounge chairs. Chase loved to play another game called "F" or "R". It meant "fake" or "real" as in women's breasts. As some woman would walk by in her bikini, he would mutter quietly "F" or "R". We would all take bets and try and guess who might be right. His British conquest walked by so I decided I would inquire and see what he said.

"F or R, Chase"?? I said wondering how he would respond to this one.
Chase responded "R...definitely".
Ryan inquired "Do you speak from experience?"
"You know it brother" said Chase as they high-fived each other.
"From what I saw two nights ago on these very lounge chairs,
Chad knows from experience too" I told him.
"Really? You saw them?" Chase asked smiling.
"Yup" was all I responded.

I don't know why I told Chase I saw them. I guess I was a little pissed he hadn't asked me out that night or seemed to act different towards me when I had a few drinks in me so I just said it. I didn't want to hurt him but in a way I did. He hurt me by leaving me out. Chase seemed indifferent about it though and almost happy about it. I wondered if he cared at all. It wasn't like he was going to meet some girl on a cruise from another country and "make it work" I guess.

It was our last night at the night club tonight. After dinner, we went back to the room to get ready. I put on a light blue sundress and wore my hair down without the braid as I had taken it out by now. I put on my favorite lotion – mango mandarin – and touched up my makeup. Chase grabbed my hand and we headed out to the club. He ordered me a margarita with lots of salt. I guess he didn't mind me drinking again tonight.

> "You smell really good Summer". "Let's have a
> great last night on the ship" toasted Chase.
> I tapped his glass and said "I agree. It's been a fun and interesting trip".
> "Let's leave this place and just hang out together
> tonight. Sound good?" asked Chase.
> "Sounds like a plan" I gladly agreed.

We finished our drink and went over by the pool and grabbed some towels to use as blankets. Then, we headed over to one of the quieter decks and found some lounge chairs and pushed them together to lay down on them covering ourselves with the towels to keep warm. It was a pretty windy night and although still warm, I was always freezing so the towels were essential for me. We looked out at the moon shining on the water and at the stars in the sky.

> "What was your favorite part of this vacation?" inquired Chase.
> "The snorkeling and horse-back riding on the beach
> were unbelievable. What about you?" I smiled.
> Chase responded "this moment is ranking high".
> "Awww, for me too" I hugged him.

Chase could always make me feel so good. Sometimes I felt like we were together. It felt so easy but it may have also been because we have just known each other forever too. We closed our eyes and just listened to the ocean. I felt like I was home because it was the same sounds that I heard in Avon-by-the-Sea. I lay my head on his chest and listened to him breathe. We must have dozed off because when I woke up and I looked at my watch and it was 3:00 a.m. I woke up Chase and we headed back to the room to make sure we were in bed before our parents woke us up the next day to pack and get ready to get off the ship.

I reflect on this vacation a lot. I only wished I had some kind of view that this would be last vacation I would ever take with my parents. I spent so much time worrying about Chase and the things that I would do together with him while my parents spent most of their time with Sam and Abbie. I know I was acting like a typical teenager wanting to hang out with friends and explore the ship and the islands but I couldn't help but have some regret in my heart. It was regret that I self-inflicted. I knew I would never have been able to foretell what would happen in just a few months in order to change my behavior but I still couldn't help but feel guilty about it. One thing that was for sure though, we all had a wonderful time together. I would really miss having these trips with our two families. The last night when I slept under the stars with Chase, I had no idea that would soon become a pattern of him being there for me sleeping and comforting me. It was the end of an era. Change was coming and there was nothing I could do to stop it…

Chapter 3

Summer's Angels

It was the 4th of July and in one month I would be turning seventeen and getting my driver's license. Seventeen is the legal age in New Jersey to get your license and I could not wait! Next year was my senior year so it would be great to be able to drive myself to school, the aquarium and wherever else I wanted to go. Just a few more weeks and freedom was upon me. Speaking of freedom, we were ready to celebrate the 4th of July. Usually my parents and I would spend the holiday with the Minella family. They always had a huge party and you could see the fireworks from their patio since the town did them out over the ocean and everyone would just hang out on the beach from the community to watch them. Of course the Minella family didn't need to go anywhere since the beach is their backyard. It was always a great time at their parties, especially the 4th of July one. Sam and Abbie always had some of their own fireworks too. Even though, they are illegal in New Jersey. They would drive over to Pennsylvania the month prior and stock up on them. Sparklers were my favorite. I knew even when I was getting older into my teens that I should be outgrowing the whole "sparkler" thing but I couldn't help it. I loved walking around with a sparkler in my hand. It just made me feel so patriotic in a goofy way. They also had these other fireworks that rolled on the ground and made flashes of white lights. I called them the "paparazzi fireworks". It was like a million cameras taking your picture. They had a huge swimming pool in their yard so we would hang out there all day on the 4th of July…swimming, barbecuing…it was a blast. Everyone in my inner circle was there – Mel, Chase and Ryan of course and Chase's buddy, Mercer.

This year though, they would be there without me. It was for a good cause though…we were going to host a fundraiser 4th of July party/dinner and the proceeds benefited the beaches and wildlife in New Jersey. It was a dinner and fireworks event - $500/plate. It was down in Cape May, NJ. My Dad had become good friends with Ron Johnson who ran the Cape May Beach and Wildlife Preservation Association. I secretly wished I was with my buddies though doing the usual festivities. Thank God for text messaging. Chase texted me every 10 minutes – "wish you were here", "not the same without you", "I just pushed Mel in the pool", "Steal some $500/plate food for me – especially anything dessert related", etc. Mel texted saying she saw Amy on the beach near Chase's house and how convenient it was that she chose that location to watch the fireworks with her friends and family. She would do anything to be spying on Chase. We were all "sweet 16" now and Amy and Chase had hooked up a few times at local parties. She was hooked on him. Amy would pretend she wasn't doing well in math so that Chase would help her. He was always an ace in math and in all honors classes for anything math related. I knew Amy was smarter than she led on. That's what I hated about her. She was always pretending and putting on a show.

The dinner location in Cape May was at one of their most beautiful Victorian Homes called the Victorian Sea Inn. It was a bed & breakfast that we had rented for the dinner party. It was a more casual place but had an adorable porch that we had set up little dinner tables on for the event. Some tables were on the porch and some were set up inside all decorated in red, white and blue. We made over $25,000 on this event for Ron's association. Dinner was wonderful and there was a lot of food. The Benson family came as well. Dr. Benson worked with my dad and Chase's father at the hospital and was also a doctor. They had a son named Robert who was a little older than Chase and I. They lived in a different town and he now went to school out of State for his freshman year in college so I didn't see him too often. I usually just saw him in the summer time at Chase's house for their parties. This year though, they didn't go to the 4th of July party at the Minella House. Robert's parents were going through a divorce and apparently his mom was at Chase's house with her new boyfriend so his father didn't want to go, understandably.

Robert was a cute guy. He was tall with brown wavy hair and he was in great shape. He worked out a lot and was a runner and athlete in a lot of sports. He was also pursuing medicine and seemed very intelligent. Robert had always flirted with me when I was younger and there were times I wanted him to ask me out but he never did. Maybe he had a girlfriend; I wasn't sure. Robert and I spoke a lot at dinner. I asked him about the divorce and made sure he was o.k. We exchanged numbers too to keep in touch. I wanted to be a friend if he needed someone to talk to with everything he was going through. Parents' separating when you are older seems harder than when you are young. It's a total change in the way you have lived your life up to that point. At least he was away in school and didn't get exposed to it too much. Robert seemed to take it in stride. He was pretty funny and made the dinner not so bad with his jokes about the waitress with a butt ten times the size of Jennifer Lopez. I didn't expect that from him.

As promised, I stole a slice of Chocolate Mousse Cake for Chase. It was really my favorite though so I figured we could share. Chase had just texted me asking if Robert was there. I told him he was. "Just so you know, he's an a★★hole" was his last text. I never understood what Chase had against Robert. He seemed like a great guy and yet any time Robert was around, Chase was mean to him. As I looked up from my never-ending text messaging, my mom caught my eye...I couldn't help but notice how radiant my mom looked tonight. She wore her hair up in a messy bun with a casual yet classy black dress and black sandals. My parents were so in love and were always holding hands.

Even Ron joked with them how they look like a bunch of high school sweethearts. They were so cute together. My parents only dated six months when they got engaged. My dad was always very conservative. He surfed and was a momma's boy. They were very protective of him. My mom was more of a free spirit. She reminded me of Mercer in that way. Their parents were very against them getting married at first but there was no breaking these two apart. They married right after school and my Mom supported my Dad through medical school. When I came along, my mom called it the beginning of the three musketeers. My parents wanted more children but it was just a fluke for them to just have me. They tried for years after getting married with no luck and even did IVF procedures with no success. After giving up and accepting that it would just be the two of them and our dog Buttercup, my mom got pregnant. I was born in the hot month of August in the summer. So, no other name seemed to work except "Summer". I was a small baby – 5 lbs, 3 oz. I guess being small was just in my genes. Chase said he liked that I was small and always carried me around. I think he also liked it so he could throw me in the pool or into the ocean!

It was around 9:30 in the evening. I just had to get myself through the fireworks going off now and we could head back home and I could meet up with my friends at least for an hour or two. Robert stood next to me and we watched them together. The fireworks celebration here was good. I still thought the finale at Avon-by-the-Sea was much better though. I lived for those huge finales with the biggest, brightest and non-stop action of fireworks display. Hopefully, this particular event would be set for another time next year so that I didn't miss out on Chase's family party. They were so much more fun than hanging out with a bunch of strangers although Robert made it bearable. I could see the clouds starting to come in and hoped rain wasn't on the way to ruin going to Chase's house.

> *"It's been fun hanging out with you tonight Summer.*
> *We should do it more often" smiled Robert.*

"I agree. You are pretty funny too. Thanks for making the night fun" I smiled back at Robert.
"Let's go", my dad said. "YES!" I responded.
"I know you were tortured here, hon. But, it was for a good cause" said mom.
"I know, I know", I responded.
"Great to see you Mr. and Mrs. Wright" Robert said politely as he shook my dad's hand and kissed my mom on the cheek.

Brownie points for my parents…I couldn't help but think. Robert was making a good impression on them. Robert gave me a hug and said goodbye.

"Such a nice young man…and, smart too!" said my parents to me as we were walking to the car.

I was only sixteen so hanging out with friends was something in my top priorities. I just wanted to hurry up and go. They understood it. They knew the beaches were important to me too, especially the marine life. I did prefer hanging out with my friends but if I could help this cause, it was important to me just as much as it was to my parents. Robert yelled to me that he hoped to see me again this summer and that he would call me and I waved good-bye. We hopped in my dad's Mercedes. It was silver and fairly new. All of the cars we had were silver for some reason. I think my dad said he just liked the way silver looked…classy. My dad was too funny with his cars. We had a Jeep though too that wasn't silver. It's red and amazing. It is such a cool car. My parents just bought it and it's for me to keep when I finally get my license next month. I cannot wait. Chase already has his license – he is six months older than me and sometimes my parents let him drive my red Jeep. It makes me so mad because it's supposed to be my car and Chase LOVES to rub that in! It was the perfect car to throw our surf boards in and go. Chase preferred a truck and said it was more of a "manly" car. I think he also wanted it because it was also easy for surfboards and he probably didn't want to get the same exact car as me.

> *"I am going to text Chase and let him know*
> *we are headed back and that we will*
> *stop by to catch the rest of the party" I told my parents.*
> *"I am sure they will all still be partying. You know*
> *how the Minella household is" said my dad.*
> *"You had fun tonight though Summer?" inquired my mom.*
> *"Yes. Robert was pretty funny too. It's a shame*
> *about his parents" I told them.*
> *"It is. Not everyone has what me and your mom*
> *have, Summer. It's unfortunate.*
> *I know Dr. Benson is struggling with it all so I can imagine*
> *Robert is too" said my dad grabbing my mom's hand.*

We were finally on the Garden State Parkway and headed back. My parents rode along holding hands. They were so cute together. It had started to rain a little. We had heard the thunder and seen the lightening so we figured a storm was coming when we left the dinner party. I was just glad it held off so they could have the fireworks. I was hoping to hop in Chase's pool though...oh well, another day. Mel texted me....she had to leave so she wouldn't be there by the time we got there. Mercer was sleeping over there though and they would be hanging out at least. I closed my eyes for a brief moment. I was hoping the ride would go fast so I could meet up with my friends. I thought about sneaking off with Chase alone and having the dessert from the party. I missed being with him tonight.

The rain started to really come down hard. My dad let go of my mom's hand so that he could have both hands on the wheel and had the windshield wipers going full blast. It was one of those passing thunderstorms that had some heavy rain and wind. I looked down at my phone and got a text from Chase that said "see you in a few...

xo". I closed my eyes again and thought about the cruise we had just gone on a few months ago and how weird Chase acted. I wanted to ask him about it. Sometimes I felt there was more to our friendship than being friends. I wondered if he felt the same way. As the drive home continued, that would be the last thing I remembered. I think I blocked out everything else or it happened too fast because the rest I can't really remember….

When I woke up, I was at Monmouth Hospital. A lot of strangers were surrounding me calling me Jane Doe. What happened? Where was I? I was able to finally speak and called out for Chase. I don't know why. He was the first person in my mind.

"Chase? Where are you? Chase…I need you."

The nurse asked me for my name.

"Summer Wright. Summer is my name. Where am I?" I said weakly. The nurse replied – "You are in the hospital. You were in a car accident ".

Suddenly I remembered. We were on our way back home from Cape May. Where were my parents? What had happened? The nurse asked me who I was in the car with. I told her it was my parents.

"My parents were in the car with me. Why, they are o.k., aren't they?" I asked frantically.

The nurse didn't really respond and seemed to pretend she didn't hear my question and ignored it.

She said a doctor would be coming in to speak to me and finished checking my vitals. My heart was racing. My wrist and head hurt and I felt sore all over.

"Am I o.k.?" I asked nearing hysterics from the panic.

The nurse said I was unconscious for over 8 hours and they were monitoring me. Eight hours? I felt like it had only been moments ago that I was sitting in the back of my dad's car on the way home. How could this have happened and why couldn't I remember it? The nurse started to leave and I started to panic and shake. How could this have happened? Where were my mom and dad? About an hour or so passed and it felt like an eternity as I lay there scared and crying. Random people would come in but no one would tell me anything and I felt kind of weak to even ask. I just wanted to go home and see my parents. The nurse who took my vitals came in said the doctor is coming in now to speak to you. She seemed like she was avoiding eye contact with me which made feel like grim news was coming my way. Finally, the doctor walked in. It was Dr. Sam Minella, my dad's best friend. He looked really tired and sad.

"Hey, kiddo" said Sam.
"Where are my parents? Am I o.k.?" I asked
anxiously wanting to cut to the chase
as my panic was getting worse and worse.

I knew in my heart they weren't....I could see by the look on Sam's face that they were gone. His eyes were puffy and red and he looked horrible. Plus, I knew they would be right here by my side in this room and I wouldn't be here alone in this bed if they were o.k. I just had some hope that there was a chance of survival. Maybe they were unconscious too and there was a chance of a miracle. Maybe they were in the trauma unit or in surgery and Sam had saved them. I silently prayed and begged God to make them o.k. while I waited for Sam to speak.

Sam didn't even look at me in the eye. He had the horrible task of telling me the news I dreaded. He held my hand and looked down and broke down crying. He told me my parents didn't make it. He said that a car had crossed the median after losing control in the rainy weather and crashed into us head on. It was a miracle I had survived with only a bump on my head and a broken wrist. My parents took the impact of the accident and never had a chance. The air bags were not enough and they died upon impact and didn't suffer. He said not to worry, that he would take care of me. He said Chase had been there since last night by my side waiting for me to wake up and is really worried about me. Sam said he had finally made him go home and rest up. I know he said more but it's all a blur. I had chills going up and down my arms as he spoke and started to whimper. The nurse walked into the room.

"Yes, Chase….he was the person you asked for when you were waking up" the nurse shared trying to break my focus on my parents for a moment even if it was brief.

Sam hugged me in that moment and I cried really hard and so did he. I was almost hysterical. I was just sort of in disbelief that my parents weren't here anymore. I was mad at God for not hearing my prayer. At any moment I was expecting them to come through that door. It just didn't seem possible that they weren't here any longer. I just couldn't believe it. This just can't be true. How could this have happened? Sam wiped my tears as I continued to sob and held my hand. He was like a second dad to me my whole life but it's never the same without your real one. It was just so unfair. Sam was used to telling people about death after all he is a doctor. But I knew this was different. This was his best friend. He was grieving too and probably in shock. Sam stayed a while and then I told him to go home. My eyes hurt so bad from crying and I felt exhausted. I told him I wanted to be alone for a while and that I would see Chase and everyone when I got home and released. I think I just went into a state of disbelief and confusion. I didn't know how to act or what to say. I couldn't handle facing anyone. Sam and Abbie picked me up the next morning and checked me out. They wheeled me out in a wheelchair and when we got to the car, I didn't even have the energy to get up and Abbie had to lift me and put me in the car. I wished I had died too. Chase and

Ryan stayed home. Abbie said she thought it would be too much for me and she was right. I didn't even want to be in a car right now. As soon as I got in it, I thought about the last ride with my parents and they were holding hands and happy.

I didn't really cry much at all right away after that initial cry. It was probably shock. I didn't really speak at all about it either. I knew what it meant to be a zombie. I wandered aimlessly and was numb. I remember it was two weeks later after getting out of the hospital, the funeral was done and we had spread my parents ashes over the ocean, and I was back home when I finally let it all out. I was almost seventeen. I had my Jeep waiting there for me but no one to tell me I couldn't drive it for two more weeks. My parents had left me everything in their Last Will and Testament. I had millions of dollars but I would have thrown it all in the ocean and preferred to live above the donut shop like Mel to have my parents back. I was……..alone; plain and simple. I didn't have any siblings and neither did my parents. Both sets of grandparents were gone. I really truly had no one in the world that was related to me that I knew of. The funeral is a complete blur. My eyes were tired. So many people were hugging me and saying kind words but I can't even remember any of them. My parents wanted to be cremated. They didn't believe in being buried in the ground. They wanted to have their ashes spread over the ocean. I just thought I would be doing this when they were old and fray not when I was sixteen years old. When we went out on the Minella's boat to spread the ashes, I remember thinking that "this is what is left – jars of ash of two people that were the loves of my life?!" Is this what life ends up like? Your ashes blow into the wind or drown in the ocean as if you never existed. It definitely wasn't fair and it just broke my heart that I would never again see my mom or dad's face, hear their voices or touch their hands. I truly hoped there was a heaven and I knew without a doubt they would be angels.

The man who drove the other car in the accident came to the funeral too. He was severely depressed and felt horrible. Of course, he walked away without a scratch. Why is it that the person that causes the accident never gets the harm? He is the only person I really remember from the funeral. He was shaking really bad when he approached me. He was a single man in his thirties. He was on his way to a friend's house in South Jersey when it happened. He broke down into hysterics when he reached me. He asked me for my forgiveness and I gave it to him. I knew it wasn't really his fault with the weather being so bad and I also knew that if I didn't forgive him, he probably wouldn't be able to ever move on. His life though would move on and he would be fine I couldn't help but think. He didn't lose anybody. It would be me that would have the hardest time moving on. I needed to forgive him though. It really was an accident. I knew he didn't do anything intentionally. I knew my parents would want me to forgive him. They were always kind, caring people and they wouldn't be happy if I was angry at him and put that guilt on him for the rest of his life. He would have guilt no matter what. I couldn't help him with that but I could at least help him feel like he had my forgiveness. I barely even cried at the funeral. I barely spoke either. I could tell no one knew what to do with me and how to help me and I didn't even care. I didn't want anyone to be there for me. I wanted to drown in my sorrows.

I just couldn't help but be in a place of self-pity though. I felt lost and alone. Abbie tried to mother me before, during and after the funeral. Stella never left my side. Mel, Chase and Mercer and other friends from school would bring me food, come over to hang out and watch movies….anything to keep my mind off what had happened. Robert came over a few times and called me every day to check in on me. I just didn't have the energy to deal with it. I had never experienced such extreme sadness. It was a sad feeling with no end in sight. It would slowly get easier to live life but the sadness in my heart had become permanent. The feeling that my parents would be calling or walking through the door at any moment never really goes away. It was so sudden and unplanned that it just never felt like there was a closure to them being gone. When a parent is sick, it's hard but at least you can say good-bye. I never got a chance and my last moments with them were spent with me worrying about Chase or my friends. I felt like I had to stop caring so much about that trivial stuff and should've put my family first. I knew I was being hard on myself. I was just acting my age at the time but I felt really guilty.

Stella was staying with me now permanently. The Minella's wanted me to stay with them at least until High School was over but I couldn't leave the house. I wasn't ready to let go. It was all I had left of my parents. I just told them no and I didn't really give them any other choice and no one really wanted to upset me further. I don't think I could take any other change and I was ready to crumble at any moment. Stella slept at my house at night and went home during the day to give me space and catch up on her own house chores, etc. Chase would sometimes sleep over too on weekends. Stella let him sleep in the bed with me. She knew he was just comforting me despite the fact that we were teenagers with hormones. That was the last thing I could even think about at that time. At this time, I couldn't even remember thinking about how I used to feel about Chase. All of those feelings were boxed up deep inside me now. I was just trying to get through each day and have the strength and courage to move forward and live life. Life went on but I wasn't ready for it to. I knew I couldn't stay in my bed forever but I didn't really feel like ever getting out of it at the time. Chase would hold me tight all night long. He hugged me when I cried myself to sleep. He is the person who really got me through a lot of my grief. We never did tell his parents that Stella let him sleep with me. Nothing ever happened. He was the closest thing I had to family.

Stella took care of my house too. She cleaned and put food in the fridge. She helped with the bills and mail. She hired a financial advisor to manage my money and pay my bills and met with him monthly to make sure everything was o.k. We ate dinner together at night and I would watch her paint and play with her dogs. I owed her a lot and I loved her so much. She was seventy five years old and was supposed to be enjoying her retirement yet she was stuck here helping me. I think she liked it though. When we went out to town, she always referred to me as her daughter. It always made me smile a little. As time would go on, she signed my report cards in school and helped me with class projects. She was the one who helped me try on prom dresses and got me through the holidays. I remember I had won prom queen and for a brief moment I thought that I couldn't wait to tell my parents. It was such a habit to share exciting news with them and they weren't here to share it with and it would bring back all my pain that I was trying to hide. I thank God every day for Stella. I needed a mom and mine was gone.

One weekend, I ventured into my house one lonely Friday night. I walked through the door inside my mini-apartment into the main part of the house and started down the hallway past all the guest bedrooms. Stella was fast asleep in one of the guest bedrooms so I tiptoed my way down the hall. I passed the door with a big "S" on it. It was my old bedroom – "S" for Summer. I hadn't been in it really since everything happened except to grab some clothes. I opened the door and looked around. I had always loved my room. It was a soft pink color on the bottom wall and the top part of the wall above the chair rail was a patterned white and beige. I loved the built-in sofa under the huge windows. Sometimes I would sleep there instead of my bed so that I could gaze outside and look up at the stars. I used to lay there and have so many dreams about the future. I would dream of being married to Chase, working as a marine biologist and surfing every weekend. Somehow the room didn't feel like mine anymore. It was the old me when I had my parents. The new me would never be the same.

I closed the door and headed down the spiral staircase to my father's office. My dad's office looked like a typical doctor's office with so many medical books and journals. The room had shadow boxes all around the bottom of the walls with a leather look inside of them. He made the room very traditional and it had pictures of horses and huntsman. The entire house was once full of life but now it felt like a museum. It just felt so lonely and sad. The serene and calm tones now just seemed cold and distant. The feeling of the house was how you feel on a rainy, cold day with gray skies. I went over to the bookshelves and on the top shelf above all the medical books was where my parents kept all the photo albums. I sat there for hours looking at them all one by one. My mom had them all done in special photo albums labeled for every year of my life. They had abruptly stopped at my 16th year of life. It didn't seem fair. The last photos in there were of the cruise we went on with the Minella family and a few photos of me surfing that my mom must've taken from our porch while she was watching. It was hard to look at them and remember all the happy times. I looked through the pictures of me as an infant, all the times at the beach with the Minella family, our vacations, my first day of school each year, and so on. The tears once again poured from my eyes and part of me said "why are you torturing yourself?" and another part of me said "you need to look…you have to remember them".

There was another album that wasn't labeled and I pulled it out. It was my parents wedding album. I don't think I had ever seen it. My parents looked so young and so happy. They were so in love with each other. Their wedding was a destination one. At the time, my grandparents were against them getting married so quickly so to everyone's dismay they planned a destination wedding in St. Lucia at the Sandals Resort. They were married on the beach in flip flops. My mom wore a strapless, simple white dress with her long blonde hair down and carried a bouquet of beautiful pink roses, my favorite. My dad wore a white polo shirt and khaki pants. When they came back, I remember my mom telling me that their parents had surprised them with a huge dinner party. They were so happy that their parents had finally accepted their love for each other. My grandparents were older and very old school. But, they came around and eventually understood the love my parents had for one another. My grandparents had all passed away by the time I was ten years old. I remember my parents commenting that they were happy they were able to see how happy they turned out and had started a family of their own. I only hoped that I could find someone to share the love like they shared some day.

I grabbed the picture of my mom holding the pink roses standing next to my dad on the beach on their wedding day and took it. I took a picture of Chase and I on the beach too. I was wearing a cheap, wooden necklace that said SUMMER on it in the photo. My parents had bought it for me and it was always so hard to find my name on anything so I treasured it. I had lost it in the ocean one summer and it was so sad for me. Chase had helped me look everywhere with no luck. I clipped the pictures inside my favorite journal that I carried with me everywhere to have the photos with me everywhere I went. I wanted the important people in my life to be close to me even if it was just a memory through a picture. I slowly made it back to my little apartment and closed the door. I crawled into bed and clutched my journal to have my parents close to my heart. I whispered to them hoping by some miracle they would hear me and know how much I loved and missed them. I wished I could see their faces one more time and hug them tightly.

A few weeks later Abbie took me to the doctor to get my cast off my wrist. It was pouring rain. The kind of summer rain where the streets were flooding at the shore, the ocean was rough with huge waves and it was very windy. You couldn't walk on the beach without sand whipping in your face. She dropped me off at my house and I thanked her and ran to my door. I didn't have an umbrella so I got soaked in that short run to my door. I watched as Abbie drove down to her house and I looked at my arms and shirt and saw how wet I was as I stood on my doorstep. I was having a rough day missing my parents. I had been crying all night and only put on a show for Abbie and the doctor that I was o.k. because I was forced to. I wanted to call Chase but he was over Mercer's house with a bunch of friends. Mel was helping her parents today at their donut shop. Stella was inside cooking. I could see her through the window with her dogs sneaking tastes here and there. I felt so alone in that moment. Everyone had a life but me.

I walked back down the steps and into the pouring rain and just stood there. I wanted to drown my misery and the heavy rain felt like my tears and it represented how I felt inside. I was completely drenched and yet I just stood there and reveled in it. Finally, I walked across the street and sat on a bench in the pouring rain looking at the rough seas. The ocean was too rough to surf and very choppy and the waves were huge. They were at least double over-head as surfers like to say – 10-12 feet or so or twice the size of a person typically. I felt so alone. I looked around at all the houses. Everyone is safe inside with their families. No one would even know that I had disappeared. No one would even notice. I could just walk into the rough seas and never reappear. I could reunite with my parents. I could put misery to an end and just be at peace. That would be the cowardly thing to do though. My parents would never want that for me. It's just how I felt in that moment. I would never do it but I couldn't help but think how easier it would be to just be gone. I couldn't even think anymore. I just sat there on the bench in the pouring rain. I don't even know how long I was there. I was freezing but I was so numb I didn't even care. I curled into a ball and just kind of collapsed and cried. The tears and the rain mixed. The rain drenched me and I just kind of felt lost in that moment and I felt the water was just sort of washing me away. I talked aloud to my parents. I asked them why they left me alone and I just sort of closed my eyes and whimpered. I held my wrist because it felt weak and it still hurt me too.

I heard someone coming but I didn't care. I just stayed there. I didn't want anyone to care about me. I just wanted to wallow in my loneliness. Chase's brother Ryan touches my shoulder frantically asking me if I am hurt. I couldn't even answer him at first. He started to get frantic screaming my name so finally I just told him I just want to be alone. Ryan runs off and comes back with Abbie and Sam. Sam wraps me in a blanket and lifts me up and brings me into the Minella house and brings me upstairs to the master bedroom and Abbie puts her arms around me and Sam and Ryan shut the door and leave.

"Summer? What were you doing? I am so sorry. I shouldn't have left you alone. This is my fault. I should've known this would be a reminder of the accident getting your cast off" shared Abbie as I just fell

into her arms sobbing. It felt so good to have a mom in that moment. I realized I needed her. I needed the Minella family and Stella.
"I just wanted to disappear with the rain today.
I'm having a bad day. It's not your fault.
It's me. I just felt alone" I confessed.
"You will never be alone" said Abbie pulling my chin so I would look her in the eyes. "We love you like a daughter Summer. I need you in my life. I don't ever want to lose you in my life. Promise me Summer. And next time you feel down, you tell me or any one of us. Do you promise?"
"I promise" I whispered shaking from being drenched.
"Let's get you in my shower and we'll get you into some clothes and I'll throw your wet ones in the laundry" said Abbie always the care-taker.

I let Abbie pretty much undress me like I was five years old because that's how I felt. I wasn't even embarrassed to be naked standing there in front of her. She pushed me into the shower and disappeared to throw my clothes in the laundry. The hot water felt so good on my skin. I felt loved. I felt like a burden to the Minella family. I felt a little bit of everything. But I did feel better. I came out of the shower and dried off and stood there in a towel and I grabbed a brush near Abbie's sink and brushed my long hair. Abbie returned with one of Chase's t-shirts and a pair of Ryan's old shorts. I would have to go commando since there was really only boys in her household and Abbie was a lot bigger than me and I would never fit into any of her things. Abbie left so I could get changed. She told me she was putting on some movies and making popcorn and we would have a little family time together this afternoon and that Ryan was downstairs picking some movies out in their theatre room.

Chase had gotten home about five minutes earlier and got looped in by Ryan and came up to his parent's bedroom. He saw his mom walking down the hall and cracked open the door to his parent's room to check on Summer. Summer was standing there getting dressed. He knew he should quickly close the door but he stood there and watched. He looked at the curves of her breasts as she pulled his t-shirt over her head. He liked that she was wearing his shirt. It made him feel closer to her. He wanted to run to her and hug her and tell her she would never be alone. He wanted to make love to her. He wanted her to be his. He just ached for her but now was not the time. Here she is in a moment of despair and all he could think about was her body and he felt shallow about his thoughts. Now definitely just wasn't the time whether his heart told him it was or not. His head knew Summer needed to heal and it would take time.

Chapter 4

Senior Year Drama

Going back to school for senior year really just a few weeks after everything had happened was extremely difficult for me. I had some options and could choose to not go back and do a home school program or start later but I knew it was inevitable and I needed to just suck it up and do it. I just knew people would stare at me and look at me differently. They would feel sorry for me and whisper. It hurt to think about it. I was really scared. I didn't even go back-to-school clothes shopping, a tradition for my mom and me. Every year, she made sure I had the latest and greatest in-style clothes. This year, I didn't even buy one thing and had barely left the house. It had been the worst summer of my life. I had no motivation to do anything but stay in bed all day. The most I had done is watch a few movies with friends that came to visit me, surf, sit on the porch, and go over to Stella's house. I spent my birthday with Stella and my inner circle. They came to me and I didn't want to go anywhere. I finally got my license and could drive my Jeep yet it just sat there in the driveway. I only drove it to take my driver's test and that was it.

About a week before school, Stella got me up early and said she wanted to spend the day with me before school kept me busy. We hopped in her car and drove and she wouldn't tell me where we were going. I just leaned on my arm and lay my head on the car door looking out the window. I wasn't much of a morning person not to mention depressed. We finally arrived in Cape May at the Cape May Whale Watch & Research Center. I knew right away what she had planned for me. I hugged Stella in the car and she told me she wanted me to get a break from reality for the day doing something I loved. There was lot of whale watching tour and companies in and around Cape May and this one might not be as extravagant as the others but Stella knew I would like this one better because they actually care about the preservation of the environment. I would rather be on this tour any day over those other ones that are there for personal gain and not giving back to our marine life. We were doing the 10:00 a.m. whale and dolphin watching cruise. When we walked onto the boat, it was clean and large. It was about one hundred feet long and was designed for non-obtrusive, up close viewing of the marine animals. Since I didn't know where we were coming, I only had my phone with me but luckily it took good pictures because I knew getting up close and personal with the animals would be amazing. The staff was friendly and very informative as well as knowledgeable. They had a snack bar on board and they had complimentary donuts and coffee, which Stella and I quickly took advantage of. There were two outdoor levels and we stayed on the main one since the top deck was where more of the children were as they were interested in the crab pool up there for the kids to check out. There were tons of dolphins as soon as we hit the open water riding along with the boat. We learned spotting techniques and other facts about how dolphins and whales actually interact with each other.

For a moment I forgot all my troubles. I was so focused on spotting dolphins and whales and just exploring their wonder. My heart was happy in this moment because it was doing something I loved so much. We were getting to a close on our boat ride and we had seen at least 30 dolphins and tons of species of birds but no whales. Just as I was about to give up hope we spotted a whale's tail as it poked out of the water. Stella and I were so excited as it's not always guaranteed to see the marine life and most people on these cruises only see dolphins. After the cruise, Stella took me to a late lunch at the Union Park Dining Room inside the Macomber Hotel. The Macomber Hotel was on Beach Avenue and was a historic house with rooms and this beautiful restaurant – the Union Park Dining Room. We both had Lobster with a side of whipped potatoes and a big glass of good old fashioned water to rehydrate from being in the sun the last few hours. This restaurant was a fine dining location and normally only opened for dinner but their executive chef had decided to open for lunch for the last two weeks of the summertime since the season was coming to an end.

> "You had fun today Summer?" inquired Stella while reaching out and grabbing Summer's hand.
> "It was just what I needed Stella. Thank you so much for a wonderful day" I quickly responded and squeezed Stella's hand back.

We drove back to Avon-by-the-Sea after our lunch and my head once again was leaning on the door staring out the window. I couldn't help but smile from a wonderful day but I dreaded school starting. Today felt like the escape I needed. I liked being around people that didn't know me or my situation with my parents. Today was the first day I felt like I fit in and was normal…thanks to Stella. It also reminded me how important marine biology was to me and I knew exactly what I wanted to do when I went to college next year. Marine Biology would be my major, not that I ever doubted it. It was really my passion and I couldn't wait to be involved with marine life for the rest of my life.

School was finally here. There was no avoiding it. The first day back was painful. The night before Chase's mom dropped off 5 shopping bags full of clothes for me. I hadn't even opened them or thanked her. When I walked into school, all eyes were on me yet no one made eye contact. Chase was over-protective. Mercer was joking constantly making it obvious he was nervous too and didn't know how to handle it. Mel never left my side unless we needed to be apart when we had different classes. It was great that they were there for me and I needed them. I was beginning to realize more and more than blood didn't always have to mean family. These people were my family. I could feel the eyes on me everywhere I went the first few days. I knew it wasn't their fault. Nobody knew what to say to me. "Should I say something to her"? "Should I not bring it up"? It was a common way to feel. I knew that this would happen. I just hated being in the situation I was in. I just wanted my parents back. I carried my journal tightly with me everywhere I went. I wanted my parent's picture with me at all times. I needed them to help me get through the days. Throughout the first few months, teachers made some calls to Stella. "Summer is daydreaming and seems disinterested in class". "Summer stares out the window and doesn't appear to be paying attention". "Summer is working too hard and seems to be taking on too much work in school". I couldn't win. I did too little or too much. There were times I couldn't focus at all. There were times when all I did was school work so that I didn't have to think about anything else but that. I was just glad colleges mainly looked at your junior year because this year was going to be a rough one for me.

I was busy cheerleading in the autumn for football so at least it kept me busy especially for Friday night games. I loved playing under the lights and the air was crisp. Chase played football. He was a running back. The quarterback was Jeff Briggs. He was a good-looking guy with brown hair and a lean, muscular body. Jeff dated one of my cheerleading friends, Stephanie. They had literally been together since 5th grade. Stephanie was a pretty girl with long brown hair and big blue eyes. Amy cheered as well but we weren't super friendly with each other. She never seemed to really like me and I could care less. I think she was jealous that I was so close to Chase. She never even told me she was sorry to hear about my parents and that hurt me too. She really was that selfish. There were football parties after the games on Friday or Saturday nights at the various football players' houses. It was something to go to and keep my mind off my problems. Chase,

Mercer and Mel went with me and we would hang out. Chase and Mercer would always get trashed. Mel and I had a drink or two but nothing crazy. Chase and Mercer always found someone to hook up with. I think Chase had kissed half of the cheerleading squad by the end of the season. One particular night, Chase was out of control. He was dancing and grinding with Amy and they kissed once or twice. It was another thing that just fueled Amy's infatuation with Chase. She always wanted to be exclusive with him. I never could understand what he saw in her. He always tried to hide it from me too but not this night…he was too wasted to hide anything. Amy was tall and pretty. She was almost his height. I was so short he probably thought of me as a child and that made me insecure. No one ever bothered to hit on me.

As the year went on, I made it through somehow and it became routine. The stares got less frequent and I started to feel like people had slowly started to forget about my troubles, although I never did. It amazed me how something horrible happens and people slowly forget unless it happened to them. I know I will never forget. My life has been impacted in a way I could have never imagined. It reminded me of 9-11 and the attack on New York City. It was so devastating yet now it's a thing of the past. The holidays were a very hard time for me in particular. It was my first holiday season without my parents. My parents had always made each holiday so special. My mom always made the house look amazing. For Halloween, we had a smoke machine and spooky music, spiders, cob webs and witches. My dad would dress up as a zombie sometimes and lay on the lawn and trick-or-treaters wouldn't even know he was there and he would scare them. He didn't care if it was a little kid or a teenager he would jump out and give you the fright of your life. Kids looked forward to coming to our house every year because of all the excitement. For Thanksgiving, we had autumn leaves and turkeys all around decorating our home. For Christmas, we had a huge tree. It was usually real and we would go and cut it down and the house smelled like fresh pine. We had lights inside and outside and they had tiny seashells on them. Even the smaller holidays like Valentine's Day or St. Patrick's Day, there was some sort of decoration in or outside of our home. I didn't bother to put anything out this year. It was too hard for me and it made me miss my mom too much. She always took such joy in doing that kind of stuff.

This year, I spent Thanksgiving with the Minella family. Stella and I went there and we helped make some of the food items to keep my mind busy and active. Cooking was always an escape for me. Although it also reminded me of my mom, it keeps you busy so that you don't have time to think while you are doing it. I made lots of appetizers, sides and desserts to bring over to Chase's house. They had a chef that actually made the meal but I didn't care. I think doing it yourself makes you feel better about eating it. You put all that hard work into it and you feel proud about it. Thanksgiving wasn't too bad and Stella got me through it all. It was my first time making chocolate mousse from scratch. It was pretty easy actually and I could tell Chase loved it. He never even looked up as he devoured it.

Christmas was harder. Stella though made Christmas amazing and tried really hard. Her son came in from Los Angeles and usually she went to him so I knew he did it because of me and they didn't want to leave me alone. It was nice to see him. Brice was there with his latest Hollywood girl – Tanya. Tanya was a buxom blonde (fake of course along with the rest of her body). She was a nice person but I know Stella sort of cringed when he brought her here for Christmas. They came for an early dinner and to exchange gifts and then were to fly out early the next morning because Brice was in the middle of working on a project and didn't have a lot of time. Stella and I were in the kitchen getting the food ready while Brice and Tanya hung out with the dogs in the living room. Tanya didn't even offer to help us. I knew that it really bothered Stella.

"All men think with their "you know what" Summer" Stella *joked with me.*
"I guess you are referring to Tanya. Seems very typical Hollywood to me but

*as long as she is nice to Brice, maybe she isn't
so bad and we shouldn't judge"*
I said trying to make her think there might be a ray of hope.

Brice liked the attention of Tanya but who knew if it would last. He was in his thirties now and didn't lead the traditional life like Stella wanted him to. He was a successful movie producer and had tons of money and fame but deep down I think Stella just wanted him to settle down and have a family. She never did become a grandmother. I guess she looked at me as her daughter or granddaughter in some ways. You couldn't help but be proud of Brice though. He was doing what he loved and he was great at it. I hoped I could say the same thing some day. Hopefully, love will find it's way too and maybe he doesn't care if it does. I think Stella hoped he would settle down but had kind of accepted that he is doing his own thing. She also never trusted the intentions of Tanya, or other girls before her for that matter. Brice was a catch with a lot of money and contacts in the entertainment industry and people were always seeking fame or money. I couldn't blame her for feeling that way. It was a good distraction for the day and helped me forget for a brief moment that it was Christmas and my parents were gone.

During dinner Brice told me about his latest film deal. They were hoping to shoot some of the scenes in NYC and NJ. I hoped it worked out because I knew Stella would love to see him more. Tanya said she was "hoping to be in it". I could feel Stella's blood boiling a little bit after that comment and I couldn't help but chuckle for a moment. I was the furthest thing from Hollywood, I thought to myself. I hated the spotlight. I couldn't stand the eyes on me when I returned from the summer back to school after my parents' accident. They were judging me for my loss and making me feel like an outcast in a way. That's how it was with fame too…you were always being judged and living every move in the public eye. I just wanted to blend in. We cleaned up the table and dishes, which of course the only thing Tanya did was bring her plate to the sink and leave into the other room. We exchanged some gifts and it was getting late. I told Stella since they were over, I would just sleep over at my house alone. I was only 10 feet away and she let me.

When I went to bed that night, I just couldn't imagine how I was going to survive the rest of my life without my parents by my side. They would never be with me for another Christmas, Thanksgiving, or Easter…they would never see me get married or have a baby. I would be on my own with it all. It broke my heart. Tears roll down my face as I lay there. I felt like a child crying for their mom scared in bed at night. That's how I felt every day. And, every day that passed, I questioned how I was going to get through my life without them. I often broke down when I was alone and cried for them. I longed for them so badly. I called Chase on the phone to come over and he snuck over when his family went to sleep and so that Stella and her son wouldn't know.

"Thanks for coming Chase. I just didn't want to be alone" I said hugging him as we lay in bed.
"I know baby. I can only imagine how hard it is on you right now. You know I am always here for you" said Chase sympathetically.
"I like to snuggle with you anyway and I am freezing. I froze running over here!" Chase laughed as he tried to put his cold toes on my legs and make me laugh.
"Stop it" I yelled laughing.
"Alright, alright" laughed Chase setting the alarm and we held each other.

I thanked God for him that night as I closed my eyes. He held me tight and hugged me all night. He snuck out early so he could get back before his parents awoke. He was my life-line. I don't know what I would do if I didn't have him. Sure I had Stella and Mel and others but my relationship with Chase meant the world to me. It always has.

Just a few days later, it was New Year's Eve. Abbie & Sam were having a huge bash at their house. Mel, Mercer and half the town would be there. Abbie had a theme of "champagne". Guests would walk into their home and right in the main entry way was a giant display of champagne glasses full of champagne. There were champagne bottles on every table and little champagne bottle favors for guests to take home. They hired a band that often played around the Jersey Shore at various clubs called "The Nerds". The Nerds are a cover band that played hits but they were absolutely awesome and sold out wherever they went. The Minella party was all anyone could talk about at school and around town. Abbie should've been a party planner for a living because she was good at it. She just had a way of thinking of everything and making it feel magical and special. I came over early on New Year's Eve to help set up. She had a catering company and party planner doing most of the work but it gave me something to do. She had a separate kitchen in her house for catering/events so the staff was in there getting all the food ready and they had set up tables and chairs throughout the lower level and created a stage area for the band to play with a small dance floor in front of it. Chase and Ryan mainly played video games all day while I helped Abbie and her staff prepare and get ready. The tables had black tablecloths on them and the chairs had gold bows. They had white and gold china on each table too. On each table, there was a vase full of noise makers, sunglasses that said the year and sparklers and other fun items to ring in the New Year. She had thought of it all.

I ran home about an hour before the party to get ready. It was a formal affair so I had purchased a black cocktail dress and heels for the party. My "LBD" or little black dress was not a typical type of dress I would wear since I was typically pretty conservative but I just wanted to be someone else tonight. It was kind of an escape for me to just be different and there was no parent around telling me the dress was to revealing. Pretending I wasn't me for a night sounded the way to go. Maybe it will help me forget my problems even if it was for a night. The dress was strapless with a plunging v-shaped plunge neck showing my ample cleavage. It hugged my body perfectly. The heels were also black with a diamond ankle strap. I wore my hair down in loose curls. I never really did that but I have to say it did look pretty beautiful. I looked like a girl from one of those Venus Catalogs. I wasn't sure if I looked too slutty or if I just looked hot or maybe I just didn't look like me and I was good with that! There were so many people coming to this party that I could easily hide in their giant home from whoever I wanted to. I kept telling myself that I am 17 years old...almost an adult and I can look like one if I want to. I texted Mel. She was also wearing a tight black dress. It was a stretchy knit dress with mesh cutouts down the side. I was with her when she bought it and she looked amazing in it. We were going to attract some attention together. Mel said she was almost at my house. Her parents were dropping her off so she could walk over with me. I looked one last time in the mirror and almost took off the dress. I didn't deserve to feel sexy and beautiful. I thought about changing into something more comfortable and less revealing as Mel knocked at the door and I let her in.

"Holy Shit Summer!' shouted Mel floored at my look.
"A good Holy Shit or a "this is way too much" Holy Shit?" I inquired.
"It's a "you look stunning" one. I can't get over it. I have never seen you look so beautiful because you always hide your body. And girl, you need to show it off more!!" smiled Mel.
"You look beautiful too" I hugged Mel.

I threw on a velvet cape to walk back over to Chase's house with Mel. It was a cold night but luckily no snow on the ground yet so I could walk in the heels. It's always colder by the ocean so even a few houses down can feel like an eternity to walk to. Mel and I were casually late. We didn't want to be the first ones there. We entered through the side since we were practically family. I didn't check-in my velvet coat just yet as I was afraid to reveal my dress. Mel didn't either. She told me she felt the same way since our dresses were both kind of revealing. She definitely had nothing to be self-conscious about. She was tall, lean and beautiful. We saw Chase, Ryan and Mercer and they told us we looked great except they couldn't really see our dresses since they were still somewhat hidden. Chase and Mercer headed off to sneak some ciompagne while Mel and I decided to finally coat check our coats. Sam and Abbie met up with us at coat check and thanked me for all of my help. Abbie told me to hide from Chase because if he were to see me in this dress she would have a lot more to worry about and I laughed. Mel and I grabbed food and mingled until it got closer to The Nerds coming on while Chase and Mercer were boozing it up and playing video games upstairs away from the actual party.

It was 11:22 p.m. now and The Nerds were about to go on. They had agreed to play from 11:30p to 12:15a or so to ring in the New Year. Mel and I still hadn't seen Chase or Mercer. I was really hoping they weren't drunk somewhere by now especially because I know how disappointed Sam and Abbie would be in Chase not to mention embarrassed in front of all their family and friends. Mel and I walked over and got a decent spot near the stage next to this group of boys from Spring Lake, a neighboring town. Abbie was very friendly with a lot of the families over there who were in her social circle. Mel and I started to hang out with them since Chase, Ryan and Mercer were still MIA. There were four Spring Lake boys and they were all very different in looks (except for two of them) but all similar at the same time. They all wore their expensive designer clothes. You could tell they had button up shirts from Dolce and Gabbana and super expensive shoes from Salvatore Ferragamo and they were all probably wealthy if their families knew Abbie anyway. Mel and I started to talk to Mike and Chris. They were twins funny enough, although not exactly identical, and we kind of found that comical to think if we were dating them how interesting that would be. I mainly talked to Chris. He was hard to miss. He was really tall and ripped. He had dark hair that was slicked back and big brown eyes. His $395.00 dress shirt was hard to miss too. He told me he played Lacrosse and lived on Ocean Avenue about ten minutes from me. I knew which house was his right away when he told me more about it because I had driven past it many times. It was a stunning estate with sweeping ocean views and beautiful landscaping. You could tell that imagination and a pursuit of excellence went into the building of this home. I could only imagine the unobstructed, panoramic ocean views in his house and it had a modern flair to it with about three levels of living from what I could tell. It was very hard to see the house from the street with tricky landscaping and a gate to enter. Chris told me that his parents worked in the entertainment industry and needed privacy not that he ever saw them. He told me they traveled from LA to NYC and all over the world and was mainly raised by nannies. Mike chimed in that the plus side is that they can pretty much do whatever they want whenever they want to because they basically have no supervision. Mike and Chris were both seniors as well.

   I could quickly tell that these boys were big trouble with big egos to go along with it. Mel and I didn't care though. There was something exciting in that. What was even better was the fact that they had no idea about me and didn't know me. I didn't need to even let them know about my parents. They just saw me for me and I liked the notion of that. Mel and Mike seemed to hit it off and as The Nerds came on, they started dancing together and laughing. Chris leaned in and whispered in my ear:

"By the way, I know we don't really know each other well but you are smoking hot".
I felt slightly embarrassed but I guess I should have expected it wearing this kind of dress.
"Thanks Chris. I am not used to wearing things like this. I typically look like your typical surfer girl ad campaign for Roxy"
I said trying to give him a picture of the "real" me.
"Maybe we should go somewhere quiet and get to know each other better" he inquired.
"I kind of want to see The Nerds" I shared. "I have been looking forward to this for months since Abbie was planning it".
"So you are a tease then? I was hoping you were a little more mature if you know what I mean" said Chris being a total jackass.

I just looked up at the stage and didn't even bother to respond. I whispered to Mel that Chris was an asshole looking for action with me after only knowing me for fifteen minutes. Mel shared what happened with Chris' brother Mike and he just gave her a look.

"What's that look for?" asked Mel.
"It's just that we are used to getting everything we want so you know he doesn't take well to the word – no" answered Mike laughing.

Mel quickly texted Mercer and Chase and told them that they were being hit on by Spring Lake brothers and to hurry up onto the floor where The Nerds were playing to rescue them. Chase and Mercer were already on their way. The Nerds had started playing and it was actually so much fun. I had already totally forgotten about Chris and his comments and was just having fun for once. Before we knew it, the countdown to the New Year had begun, courtesy of The Nerds. Mel and I embraced each other as we started to count along. I was truly excited for a New Year and new beginnings. Chase and Mercer pushed through the masses of people trying to reach Summer and Mel as the countdown began.

10 – 9 – 8 – 7 – 6 – 5 – 4 – 3 – 2 – 1 HAPPY NEW YEAR!!!!!!!!!!!

Chase made it in the nick of time with Mercer still several feet behind him and grabbed Summer and kissed her on the lips cutting off Chris in the nick of time. Mercer made it finally too but Mike already had his lips on Mel and he couldn't help but laugh at her shocked look.

Chase literally froze when they stopped kissing and got a good look at Summer. He was thinking about really giving her a true kiss when he couldn't help but notice her in that little black dress.

"I see you've met my girlfriend Summer" Chase said to Chris.
"Wow, I had no idea you guys were dating. Sorry dude. Didn't intentionally try to make any moves on your woman" replied Chris as Chase put his arms around Summer.
"No biggie dude. Just off limits if you know what I mean" smiled Chase.

I went along with the part and couldn't help but think of that brief kiss we had shared just moments earlier. It actually felt natural and kind of perfect. I also thought thank God he had made it in the nick of time. Not that kissing Chris was a bad thing but he definitely didn't deserve it. Chase, Mel, Mercer and I danced the rest of the night to The Nerds until they wrapped up their set and everyone started to leave. Chris came up to me before he left to apologize.

"Sorry about before Summer. I had no idea you were with Chase" said Chris and he looked like he meant it.
"It's o.k. We actually have more in common than you think Chris. We both have parents that aren't around. Different scenarios and I won't get into it but I can kind of understand where you are coming from" I confided to him.
"You're a cool chick Summer. Got to jam, we have another party to go to" said Chris as he grabbed Mike and headed out front where a car service was already waiting for them.
"Must be nice" I thought to myself but I could tell that Chris had a lot of issues. I felt sorry for him as I watched them walk out acting like they didn't have a care in the world.

Mel was sleeping over so we went to the coat check and retrieved our coats and Mercer and Chase walked us home. Chase joked that he wanted to make sure Mike and Chris weren't waiting for us. They walked us to the door and gave us hugs. Chase yelled "bye girlfriend" to me and I yelled back "bye boyfriend" and we smiled. Mel and I walked into my apartment and cracked up about the night's events and then we quickly got comfortable putting on pajamas and took off our make-up and made popcorn, grabbed some sodas and pulled out a stack of movies for a movie marathon.

"Here's to making the rest of senior year as memorable as New Year's" said Mel toasting my glass of Pepsi. "Cheers" I replied and we started a movie marathon of all of our favorite John Hughes movies starting with

"Sixteen Candles". We would just sleep New Year's Day away and stay up watching movies. We were both much too awake from all the excitement.

The months soon pass and somehow Spring-time was here already. The whole school year was really a daze as I reflected back. I couldn't wait for it to end in a way but I also didn't want it to end. Change was something I didn't want any more of and felt I couldn't handle. I just needed to get through prom and graduation and I tried to get through each day just because I had to. It was really all a blur. Senior year should be some of the best times in one's life but mine will never be that way despite a lot of fun memories too like New Year's Eve. I felt lost and alone really and just wanted to go back to the way things were. At least I could focus on some of the school year-end activities and it was kind of exciting to sort of jump into adulthood too…college, being able to vote….it was a new life about to begin for sure. Soon Chase, Mercer & I would be doing dawn patrol and night surfing. I couldn't wait for that. Surfing was such an escape for all of us. Once you start to surf, you just never stop. It becomes a part of you. Anyone who does it knows exactly what I mean. Right now though, my focus was on school and finishing up high school. Next up was prom and that was an interesting time…

I had always envisioned in my head that Mel would go with Mercer and I would go with Chase. The four of us were so inseparable that I just couldn't see it any other way. None of us were in serious relationships either so it just made sense. Mercer had already asked Mel a few days ago. They have always been just friends and are always each other's back-up plan for anything important. I thought about asking Chase because prom was just a few weeks away and he hadn't asked me but was hoping that he would ask me being the guy and all. It was getting to that time and everyone was planning their dates and dress/tux shopping. I still had no idea what I was going to do. It just added more frustration and confusion to my already complicated mind. I invited Chase over one night after school and was trying to work up the courage to ask him. I wanted to get to him before Amy did too.

It was a Thursday night and Chase had come over to do homework with me. I was trying to see how I was going to bring the prom subject up and then see if he would ask me and if not, I would ask him. My heart was racing. I hated this kind of stuff. I've always been an avoider. I was gathering my thoughts when he got a phone call from Stephanie, Jeff's girlfriend. "What could she possibly want with Chase??" I thought in my head as I saw her name show up on his phone's screen. He got up and paced a little and was listening to her and sounded like he was trying to comfort her. Then, I could tell it was something I dreaded…she asked him to the prom. I never would've expected this. I could also tell Chase was put on the spot and kind of glanced over at me after she asked but he said "sure, we'll have fun and don't worry about anything". I was really disappointed and my heart ached a little but I didn't tell him. I wanted to tell him so badly. I always did that to myself with Chase…there were so many times I wanted to tell him that I felt something more than friendship between us but never had the nerve. Chase told me that Jeff and Stephanie had broken up and she didn't know what to do about prom and asked him. I didn't tell Chase I was hurt. I didn't have any right to make him go with me. I just hoped he would've asked me. I felt so let down and disappointed.

*"I don't know who I am going to go with. Mercer
and Mel are going together as friends.
Maybe I should ask Robert Benson. He is back from
school next week and will be around"
I said to Chase hoping for guidance.
"Robert can't do it. I don't think he will be around. I
am pretty sure he is going away that weekend"
Chase said to me irritably.
"Oh" I said disappointed.*

I felt alone once again. It was true that I didn't make any attempts to get dates and no one dared ask me out because of all I had been through with the exception of Chris from New Year's since he knew nothing about me and couldn't judge me. So, I guess what else should I expect...I had put myself in this situation...I should've had the strength but I didn't. It just made me feel more depressed... I wanted to say to Chase that I had wanted to ask him but I didn't want him to be forced to reconsider. Asking me should be something he "wanted" to do...not something I forced him into doing through guilt. After Chase left I cried myself to sleep. I felt so pathetic. I just didn't want to go if it wasn't with him. I thought about not going at all in fact.

When I got to school early the next day on a Friday morning, I saw Jeff Briggs in the cafeteria.

"Hey Summer. How is it going?" asked Jeff nicely.
"I'm good. How come you are at school so early?
I am only here because I have some
work I have to do that I didn't finish last night" I told him.
"I just needed to get in unnoticed and didn't feel like
facing anyone today" Jeff told me solemnly.
"Why? What's going on?" I asked concerned even
though I knew why already because of Chase.
"Stephanie and I broke up. I don't even know why. We've just
been fighting lately and she said she couldn't even remember why
we were together anymore and that was it" Jeff shared.
"I'm so sorry Jeff. I know you guys have been going
out for like forever now" I replied sadly.
"That's the thing Summer...I need to ask someone to the prom
since I am not going to go with her and we have always been
friends. Do you have a date yet or would you consider
going with me?" Jeff asked smiling.
"Wow, sure! That would be great" I said pleased as I now had a date.

I was relieved to have a date despite the circumstances of Jeff and Stephanie's break-up. I told Stephanie when I saw her later just because I felt weird and she said it was fine. She said her relationship with Jeff was over and she was moving on. I just hoped she didn't think Chase was who she wanted to move on with. The whole thing felt so strange. That weekend was dress shopping time. I needed to get something and decide what I wanted to wear. After several stores, I picked out a beautiful long gold gown. It had a sweetheart neckline and was a sequined, strapless, slim-line gown with a beaded and crystal band around the waist. It was gorgeous and Stella had come with me and cried when I had it on. I knew that was the right dress by her reaction. I felt beautiful in it too. Mel and I had planned a day of beauty during the day of prom and got the works…manicures, pedicures, hair and make-up. It was a lot of fun. I wore my hair up and even I didn't recognize myself in the mirror. Mel was wearing a red, chiffon mermaid gown that was strapless and fitted to her body. She looked amazing. Mercer was going to the fall to the floor when he saw her. Of course, I wouldn't be there to see his reaction though and it made me sad that I wasn't going in the limo with my friends. Chase and Stephanie would be going with Mel and Mercer in a limo together. Since I was going with Jeff, I went with him and a few of his football friends. It was fine but it just didn't feel the same and it definitely wasn't the way I wanted it to be or had imagined it to be. But I guess that's how my life was turning out…nothing went as I thought it would go.

Jeff came and picked me up and Stella snapped some pictures and we headed to the limo. We were the first to be picked up and then made the rounds picking up everyone else. Jeff told me I looked amazing and he meant it…He told me I was stunning and that he had always thought I was beautiful. It made me feel good. He looked great too. I was trying to hold all of my emotions in and just have fun. As we stopped at each house, I had to force myself to smile for all of the pictures. Everyone was in great moods and we all looked great too. Some of the guys were drinking beer from a beer ball that they brought into the limo. I guess the party had begun! I stayed away from it since I am not a beer drinker. Plus, I wasn't in the mood and sometimes a drink can make someone more emotional and I certainly didn't need any more emotions. We finally arrived at the prom. It was being held at a local hotel's banquet hall. They had decorated it beautifully with magnificent flower arrangements everywhere. We didn't have any real theme. We just did a DJ and it was a traditional prom-type of dance. I just couldn't wait to see my friends once we got there. It took a while to get in as they had a photographer photographing each couple as they arrived. We made it to our table and put our stuff down and started to mingle. When I arrived at our table, I saw Mel and Mercer right away and ran over to them.

"Mel, you look absolutely beautiful" I said sincerely.
"You do too, Summer. Wait till Chase sees you,
he is going to die!" she said excitedly.
"You look amazing Summer! Really hot!"
said Mercer and he gave me a kiss.

Chase saw Summer across the room and couldn't believe his eyes. She was more beautiful than he had ever seen her. He felt bad that he didn't just ask her like he wanted to. "I am such a coward" thought Chase. It would have been the perfect night yet now he was here with Stephanie. Stephanie was a beautiful girl in her own right but so far all night all she had been doing was crying over Jeff and had told Chase she missed him. He felt bad for Stephanie. He was trying to cheer her up and have a good time. Chase was so afraid to hurt Summer after all she had been through but his heart ached for her. Chase couldn't take his eyes off of Summer as he walked over to Mercer, Mel and Summer.

"Wow Summer. You look stunning" said Chase adoringly.
"You look really good too like I knew you
would" I said and gave him a kiss.
"How is Stephanie doing?" I inquired.
"Missing Jeff badly" said Chase.

We all danced together and had a good time. I felt like we had all gone together for a moment and forgot all about my date. Dinner was being served so we headed back over to our tables. Jeff and I ate dinner and made small talk. He seemed distant and unhappy. I mainly was on the dance floor with Mel most of the night while Jeff hung out with his football buddies. A slow song came on and Jeff asked me to dance. His football friends joked about her good we looked together. Stephanie was nearby so I knew they were trying to piss her off by saying it too. We did actually look good together though but my heart would never be into Jeff and I could tell his was definitely somewhere else too. As Jeff and I were slow dancing, I could see Jeff glancing over at Stephanie. I knew he was hurting.

"Jeff, I need to tell you something. Chase told me that Stephanie is having a really hard time and misses you really badly" I confided in him.
"Really?" Jeff said with hope in his voice..."I
have to confess. I feel the same way.
I'm sorry Summer. I hope I am not ruining your night".
"Not at all" I said as I moved him over so that we
could dance closer to Chase and Stephanie.
As I got close enough, I tapped Chase on the
shoulder..."Let's switch partners"
and I pushed Jeff and Stephanie together.
"It's that bad huh?" asked Chase as he put his arms around me.
"Yes. It's pretty sad. Two people that obviously
want to be together but both are afraid to
just go over and let the other know" I said.
Chase couldn't help but think he knew how Jeff and Stephanie felt.

I couldn't help but think I was the same way. I had wanted to go to the prom with Chase but was afraid to ask him. I just didn't want to put him on the spot, as Stephanie had. I wanted him to "want" to go with me.

> *"Looks like your move worked" said Chase pointing to*
> *Jeff and Stephanie who were kissing each other*
> *as Chase and I smiled at each other.*

I didn't mind. I was glad that they were together. The music stopped and the DJ made an announcement…it was time for Prom Queen and King. Mr. Lizowski, one of our teachers, went up to the microphone to make the announcements. I knew I could possibly win. People could vote for anyone at all in our school. There weren't any campaigns like you see at other schools so you really had no idea who it would end up being. Prom King was announced first. It went to Jeff. I had a feeling it would. Pretty typical – high school quarterback gets Prom King but Jeff was a great guy and not your typical popular guy. He definitely deserved it. His smile was bigger than ever but I think it was mainly because he appeared to have made up with Stephanie, who was cheering him on. Then they announced Prom Queen next. I couldn't believe it - it was me. Chase gave me a kiss on the cheek as I went up to get my crown. It was a great feeling. I really didn't expect it. I thought for sure Stephanie would have gotten it. Jeff and I went up and got our crowns and did our dance together. Jeff told me we were destined to go to prom together since we were Prom King and Queen. I could see Chase watching me as I danced and he gave me the thumbs up and then walked out towards the lobby to probably get a break or sneak some drinks because I could tell he had been doing that all night too.

The prom was coming to a close and Jeff and Stephanie were pretty much hanging out now. I felt like a third wheel in a lot of ways even though Jeff made sure to be a good date to me still.

> *"Listen Jeff, if you don't mind, I am just going*
> *to head out with some other friends.*
> *I think you and Stephanie should just head out*
> *together in the limo" I told him.*

> *"Summer, I came with you and I will take you*
> *home" said Jeff being a gentleman.*
> *"I know but I know how much you guys love*
> *each other and I am just so glad*
> *you were able to work it out so go out together*
> *and enjoy the night" I told him.*

Jeff thanked me. I knew in my heart that is what he really wanted to do. I would just go home with my friends. It's what I wanted to do in my heart too. I hadn't seen Chase in a while and wanted to tell him I would come home in their limo but my phone was acting up and I couldn't get a signal. I looked out in the lobby where I could see him drinking something concealed in a bottle that obviously wasn't water. Amy was there with him drinking heavily too. I went to walk up to them to see if I could hop in Chase's limo with my friends since Stephanie wasn't going with them any longer but as I walked up I saw Amy lean in and kiss Chase. Gross! I couldn't help but think. She obviously kissed him but he didn't seem to do anything to stop it. I didn't know what to do and I ducked into the ladies room and into a stall. I didn't want to call Stella. She was older and would be all worried and nervous that something happened if I told her I needed a ride. I didn't see Mel and Mercer around anywhere either. I could've just called them but I just felt like I didn't want to go with them now. Jeff and Stephanie were together. Mel and Mercer would go with Chase in the limo. Now, if Amy went in the limo too, I felt weird. I decided on a whim to call Robert Benson as my phone signal came back in the bathroom of all places.

> *"Hey, Robert? It's Summer" I said to Robert.*
> *"Hey! Isn't it prom tonight?" Robert asked confused.*
> *"Yes, how did you know?" I inquired.*
> *"Chase told me. Are you having fun?" he asked me.*
> *"Sort of. I was wondering if you were around*
> *tonight. I know Chase mentioned you were*

> *going away this weekend. If you were around
> though, I was thinking of asking you
> to come pick me up at the hotel here?"*
> *"Away? What would make Chase think that?
> I just got back from school. Weird.
> I'll gladly come get you. Did Chase leave you there
> or something?" asked Robert concerned.*
> *"No, I didn't go with Chase...it's a long story" I told him.*
> *"I thought you guys were going together. OK. You
> want to go out for ice cream or something before
> I bring you home? You'll look smokin' in your prom
> gown there!" Robert asked affectionately.*
> *"Sounds great. Come now and I'll wait out front" I told him.*

I went outside and stood off to the side so none of my classmates would notice me. I could see Jeff and Stephanie and their friends heading into the limo and out into the night. I texted Mel and told her I was leaving with Robert. Robert arrived and picked me up and I made it out of there. Mel texted me back and said "you go girl". She was always making something out of nothing. Robert was just doing me a favor.

> *"Jesus Summer. You look absolutely beautiful" shared
> Robert as he pulled up and opened the car door for me
> and by the stunned look on his face, he meant it.*
> *"Thanks. You know I was going to ask you actually
> to go with me to prom not that a college boy
> wants to go back to the prom again" I told him.*
> *"I definitely would've gone! I wish you would've asked me especially
> seeing how you look!" said Robert adoringly.*
> *"I just would have assumed you would've gone
> with Chase though" said Robert.*
> *"No, he didn't ask me. I wanted to go with him.
> I kind of thought it would've been*

Chase and I along with Mel and Mercer but he ended up getting asked by someone else and so did I so it is what it is".

Robert and I stopped at the ice cream store around the corner from my house and ate outside. We could see some of the limos driving by as we sat there. Chase, Mel and Mercer were in the limo on their way home and drove past. The limo stopped in front of us and Mercer rolled down the window as they saw me sitting outside the ice cream shop with Robert.

"Summer baby" yelled Mercer.
"Hey guys" I said. "Have fun?"
"What are you doing here Robert?" asked Chase.
"I went to pick up Summer. She needed a ride" said Robert.
"Jeff and Stephanie are back together you know so I felt weird going with them and I thought maybe you were going home with Amy" I yelled to Chase.
"Have fun!!!" yelled Mel as the limo driver started to pull away.
"See ya!" I yelled back.

Chase was pissed at Summer for not going back in the limo with them and he would never go home with Amy. Why would she think that? They had an extra spot. And, why would Summer call Robert of all people. It hurt him a lot but he didn't share it with anyone, not even Mercer. In the meantime, Robert and I finished our ice cream and he brought me home and Stella was waiting for me. What a strange night. At least I survived it and made prom queen. It wasn't a total loss. And, I did feel good for once, even if the night didn't go the way I wished it would've. Plus, I always had fun with Robert. He was a fun guy and I was glad to hang out with him for a while.

School was finally coming to an end. We got our yearbooks and were making the rounds getting people to sign them. There were pictures throughout of Chase, Mercer, Mel and I. There were a lot of great memories. I took school ending really hard in a lot of ways.

I had gotten used to the routine and didn't want any more change in my life. The last week of school there was a picnic for the afternoon and they had a DJ and we all hung out. It felt like a mini-prom in a way and I treasured hanging out with my three best friends that day. We did graduation later that week on the football field at the school. Everyone's parents were there to cheer them on. It was a hard day for me, although Stella sat proudly watching me. Later that night, the Minella family had a huge graduation party for Chase and for me too. It just felt so awkward although I knew how hard they tried and wanted me to feel like a part of their family. My whole life I practically was a part of their family anyway. It was all of the Minella extended family there and I knew them all from growing up going to their parties but my parents weren't there and I felt like I was in a room of strangers without them. I couldn't wait for that party to be over. It was mentally exhausting for me to endure it in a lot of ways. I still felt most of the time like hiding out in my bed and being alone. At least school was over and it was summer break now. And, it was my last break before college and real life started. None of us really worked that summer. We just had part-time jobs and we mainly hung out at the beach, surfed and spent time at the Minella house swimming and barbecuing. It was overall a great summer with the exception of the 4th of July just because I missed my parents so much and that was the day I lost them.

I had gotten my wish and was able to attend the Minella family 4th of July party again that I had missed last year. But, I couldn't help but be reminded that it was this dreadful day that stole two soul mates from me. Not even the sparkler that I cherished so much in my hand would make me forget what had happened. I couldn't believe a year had passed since their death. The fireworks this year were the best show I had ever seen though and I thought for a brief moment it was a message from parents that they were there making it special for me. Chase held my hand as the fireworks went off.

"I love you Summer. I know this is a hard day for you" said Chase.

"I love you too Chase" I said as I leaned into him and he hugged me.
"I am just so glad I didn't lose you that night"
shared Chase and I just held back tears.
Abbie watched Chase and Summer from the
distance and asked Sam "are you
thinking what I am thinking"?
"I've always thought it" replied Sam thinking
that there was a little spark there
between his son and his best friend's daughter.

Chase was the only one I wanted to get me through the pain I felt that day. He really is my best friend. The future was upon both of us and I couldn't help but wonder how it would all end up. I just knew I was lucky to have him by my side. I never wanted to lose him in my life. As we watched the fireworks, I just took a deep breath and got lost in Chase's arms silently telling my parents how much I missed them.

CHAPTER 5

"Summer" School

Life had gone on like it always does. I had somehow made it through my senior year and now high school was finally over and college was about to begin. All of my closest friends had gotten into Monmouth University. It was a local school and private university but most importantly had a great marine biology program. Not to mention it was situated only one mile from the beautiful ocean. I loved that Monmouth University offered high-quality, innovative academic programs. You studied in historic buildings and modern ones and yet it was still a part of a very friendly and supportive community. It was only about a thirty minute drive from Avon-by-the-Sea. It was also always in the Princeton Review as one of the best colleges. I was proud and happy to go there. Despite all those reasons the school is so great, part of me wondered if all my friends went there to comfort me. I didn't want to be seen as a burden or different because of the accident that stole my parents but inevitably I was. I don't think I could've lived without my friends or their support and was secretly glad they would all be with me for this ride. I had my heart set on marine biology and couldn't wait for it to begin. That was something I knew for sure. I couldn't ever imagine pursuing anything other than that. Mel was in the program with me too which meant we would go through it together, and that definitely made me more confident as a student. Chase was going to pursue a finance degree although my party boy was barely ever in class. Mercer majored in education. That just didn't surprise me one bit. Mr. Surfer Dude wanted to teach so he could have his summers off to lifeguard and surf. Mel met Ronnie freshman year. He was in the marine biology program as well. I knew Mel really liked him because wherever Mel was, Ronnie was. They both worked with me part-time at the aquarium. Amy of course was at the university too. I knew she would follow Chase wherever he went. She was a Theatre Major and I couldn't help but think that it suited her. She was after all, pretty theatrical in her attempts to get Chase.

    Freshman year was off to a start. We made new friends and joined sports, clubs and activities. It was a new sense of freedom. Other than the classes you were forced to take for your major or to graduate, you had some freedom too in picking electives that interested you. It was a new kind of life. I loved to walk around the campus and just take in its' beauty. Chase spent the first half of the year with Mercer pledging a fraternity so Mel and I didn't see as much of them as we would've liked. I was never really a sorority type and neither was Mel so we passed on that option. It was kind of comical to watch Chase as a pledge. The frat members forced them to do some pretty funny things and they had to carry around a paddle with them everywhere they went and it was decorated with the their fraternity insignia on it. They were very secretive about it as anything they did had to be kept under lock and key so no one really knew what they went through to get into that fraternity. I mainly think they joined because they are both very social and it was a way to have instant access to friends and partying. I did try out for the Monmouth University Cheerleading Squad and made a spot as a flyer on the team. My weekends were spent cheering at home games and Mel and Ronnie would often come and watch along with Stella. It was a lot of fun. I was surprised Chase didn't join the football team but he told me that as much as he liked it in high school, his knees were really bothering him from the sport and he didn't really want to get involved again other than going to the games. There were several really cute football players too. A lot of the players were in the same fraternity as Chase so he knew them as well. They all called me "Chase's Summer". I wasn't sure why.

Amy joined a sorority too and they were the sister sorority to Chase's fraternity. I couldn't help but think that was pretty convenient for Amy since I knew she still liked Chase. It was also another reason why I didn't pledge. I didn't want to be considered a "sister" to Amy. That was never going to happen. It kind of annoyed me though that they often had mixers on weekends which are parties where only that sorority and fraternity members could attend. This meant Mel and I couldn't hang out with them and Mel and I were on our own most weekends. Once Chase and Mercer were officially in the fraternity though, they had more time to hang out with us too thankfully. They still had their own events and activities with the frat but they were back to themselves and less cult-like after pledging was over. I still felt though like Chase had a new life for himself. He had a new set of friends and a new set of girls pining for him. It made me feel like we were growing apart in some ways and that made me really sad. I didn't want to lose him in the way we had been together growing up and in high school. He was everything to me and now I had to share him with everyone.

Since Chase and Mercer knew most of the football players, they often partied with us after football games which was so much fun. Everyone was always hooking up but I felt like none of them were ever interested in me and I could never figure out why. "Chase's Summer, what's up girl?" they would say as I walk through the door into any party or game or class. I felt like Chase had told them something about me and it made me mad inside. I didn't want everyone to know about my parents. I wanted a fresh start and I couldn't help but wonder if he told them about my situation and everything I had been through to make them leave me alone. I never asked any of them because I didn't want to break down to them about my situation. It was locked in my heart now and only those who really knew me would see that side of me.

It was November already and I had cheered at the home

Thanksgiving Football game and then ate Thanksgiving dinner at Chase's house with Stella. After dinner, I was tired and it was nighttime by now and I came home to hop in the shower when I looked at my surfboard leaning on the wall. The water was cold by now but I had a whole array of wet suits. I texted Chase and Mercer and asked if they were up for night surfing. Mercer said he was out of town and couldn't but Chase just asked me "why"? We only went out when we had a lot on our mind so I guess he just wondered what was on mine.

"How about I just come over and we can talk?" texted Chase.

I paused before responding. Now he didn't want to even night surf with me anymore. I felt like things were getting more and more distant. The Chase I know would never pass this up. He treasured it or so I thought.

I finally just texted back "forget it – it's kind of late anyway. Night xo"

I didn't wait for him to respond and just turned off my phone and put it on the charger. I hopped in the shower and it felt really good. I was half-frozen from cheering all day at the game and still had my uniform on at 8:00 p.m. since I had gone straight from the game to the Minella's house for Thanksgiving dinner. I stayed in the shower for a long time and kind of just let the water drown out my thoughts. I felt like crying. I wasn't sure why. My parents…Chase…My life. Where was I taking my life? I thought college would make me so happy and I questioned everything I did. I just wasn't happy. Mel was always with Ronnie now. Chase and Mercer were always doing their own thing and hitting on girls all the time. I needed to let someone in too. I really never have dated anyone seriously. I was giving myself permission to put myself out there.

I pulled on my nightgown, brushed my teeth and dried my wet hair with the hair dryer because I was still freezing. I went to lay in my bed when I saw Chase already in it.

"Well, this is a nice surprise" I said kind of startled. I couldn't help but think I am practically naked too in my nightgown.
"I just wanted to check on you Summer. I was worried about my girl" confided Chase.
"I am o.k. Just wallowing in self-pity today" I said as I slid into bed with him.
"Are you staying over?" I asked.
"Hell yes" said Chase "So what's going on with you?".
I turned to face him and said "I just feel a little lost in college. I thought I would be happier I guess. I feel like you, Mercer and Mel have found your place here. You've developed friendships outside of our circle and I am really happy for all of you but it just hasn't happened for me in that way".
Chase responded "Summer, you don't need anyone else but us and you have developed friendships with people in your major, other cheerleaders and the football players. You are also a part of their circle now too".
"I guess" I continued "but I feel alone a lot. Maybe I need to start dating. I guess I blocked that part of my life out and Mel has Ronnie. You and Mercer are always hooking up and I feel like I want to find that part of my life too. Maybe that's what's missing. Maybe it isn't. It could just be that I still have so much grief in general and it's really just that instead. I don't really know. It's why I thought about going out tonight surfing. Not sure it would've helped though. I don't really know what's bothering me I guess except that I miss the four of us the way we always were but I know that can't last forever I guess".
"It will last forever Summer because you are stuck with us forever. Especially with me Summer. You are never going to lose me in your life. I can promise you that".
"OK. Just checking I guess" I said closing my eyes and drifting off to sleep.

Chase just lay there next to Summer and watched her sleep. "I need to grow up" he thought. This isn't what Chase had planned on happening with Summer. He didn't want her to date other people. He wanted to date her. Why couldn't he just say it to her. He let every opportunity slip through his fingers and he felt the pressure of his frat brothers to hook up and not look like he was whipped on some girl. He made it clear though that Summer was off-limits. He knew there were a lot of cool guys he had gotten to know better and they could easily impress Summer. Since they were brothers, they had a pact with not going after certain girls and Summer was Chase's "stay away from her". He knew he was sabotaging her in a way. Why couldn't he just grow up and be a man and go for what he wanted in his heart his whole life. Summer was the total package. She was so beautiful with her blue eyes and long blonde hair. But her body just drove him insane. He liked sleeping with her to get as close as he could to her body. He wanted her so bad but he knew if he ever crossed that line, there was no turning back. Instead, he had made her feel unwanted and sad. She didn't need any more hurt in her life. He had to make some decisions and get his act together to get to a place where he felt ready to tell her once and for all.

As freshman year passed in college, I had started to date a few people here and there. I had found that since the death of my parents, I was very guarded. I never let anyone get too close to me. I wasn't sure why except that my heart was still broken. I decided though to be happy. I think ultimately I just wasn't giving myself permission to actually be happy in my life. I kept punishing myself for my parents' death. I couldn't ever forget them but I couldn't keep punishing myself over and over again. Sophomore year I had finally started to find acceptance. I was enjoying my major and spending tons of time with Mel, Ronnie, Chase and Mercer which made me really happy. We had game nights and went to clubs and just hung out in general. I had cheered through football season and had a blast. I spent a lot time with Stella and she was remodeling part of her house so I helped her with painting and things that I knew were hard for her. The year flew by and I was finding my place and enjoying myself for once. Things with Chase had gotten different. He wasn't going out without me as much anymore. I felt like we were together but he would never say it or act upon it. I wanted him to but I never did it either so I guess I am not one to talk. I started to really think that I may find my ultimate state of happiness soon. But just as I was getting to a good place with myself, Chase broke news to us one night when we were playing card games at my house. Mel, Ronnie, Mercer and a few others were over. Chase said that he was leaving to study abroad for Junior Year. It was something I know his parents had wanted for him when he was in high school to get a better view on the world but I didn't want him to go. Worst part though, I also couldn't believe it was a whole year versus only doing a semester abroad.

"Why would you go for a year? I thought it was only possibly a semester abroad" I said deflated.
"It was something that my parents wanted for me really. My mom really feels that it takes about three months or so just to acclimate to living in a foreign country and that it would be a better experience for me to be there for about eight or nine months to really get more knowledgeable of the culture" shared Chase.
Chase Continued "It's only a temporary situation and I'll be back for Senior year and plan on staying here after that permanently. I know I will miss everyone but it's something I need to do and it will be good for my career down the road".

I couldn't believe Chase was leaving me. I knew it wasn't forever and with technology we would talk every day but I would miss him terribly. And, he had suddenly gotten so motivated. It wasn't the "no cares in the world" boy I knew. He was growing up. It made me feel far away from him because I felt like I wasn't growing up. I was stuck in the same place. About a month later Chase left for Europe. He didn't even stay for the Summer. It was such a hard goodbye for me. I knew he would return but a lot can happen in a year and I would no longer be around to make sure he was o.k. and our relationship could suffer. It scared me so much but it only made me appreciate Chase in my life even more. I didn't want to be apart from him. That I could say for sure. I kept myself busy taking summer classes and working to keep my mind off things.

Before I knew it, my junior year was off to a start. Mercer spent more time with his frat brothers now that Chase was away. I felt back to being alone again. I really relied on Chase to be there for me and now he was gone. I would sit around my apartment listening to Richard Marx – "Right Here Waiting For You". I liked to wallow in my pity for Chase. I finally decided I couldn't let myself get that depressed again and tried to get more involved and really throw myself into school like I had done over the summer when Chase first left. My major required classes now filled my schedule and I wanted to really focus on acing those classes and doing well. I studied and did school work all the time and was often found in the library. Finally I had started to date someone. I think mainly because I was bored and never knew where I stood with Chase. I could see from social media that there tons of pictures of him around Europe with girls. I wasn't sure if they were "with" him or just friends but I just couldn't be sure. I felt like he was moving forward and I was still in the same place. I had to put myself out there. Most recently on and off about mid-Junior year or so I had been dating Brad. Brad lived on campus and was actually from North Jersey. He was nice and fun but there was something I couldn't put my finger on about him. Plus, I constantly pushed him away and he just took it. I never understood why he bothered with me and decided to deal with the crap I gave him. I guess I just didn't want to focus all my energies on some guy and just focus on school. I still kept in touch with Robert Benson too. He was pre-med so he was super busy. He would hang out with us in the summers and on an occasional weekend when he could. His parents had been divorced for a while now so he had to split up a lot of his time when he was around with them so it was hard to get together. We had spoken a lot on the phone throughout the years though. He was very kind to me when I lost my parents and I tried to help him deal with the divorce. It was nice to talk to someone not in the inner circle. He knew me in a different way which wasn't a bad thing. Plus, I knew my parents had really liked Robert.

School was going well. Deep down, I wasn't really the classroom type though and preferred to just be at the beach surfing in the nice weather or at the aquarium where I worked part-time with Mel and Ronnie. Plus, I found it a little hard to concentrate sometimes with everything I had been through. Thankfully Mel was around me 24/7 and it was fun to watch her with Ronnie...Ronnie and Mel began to fall in love. The more time we spent together at the aquarium and school, I could see them growing closer. They were so cute together and I was happy she found someone special. They wanted me to drop Brad and find someone I really wanted to be with. I just couldn't be bothered right now. Brad helped me keep my mind off Chase. I told them I needed to finish school first and then I would worry about love. I should stop stringing Brad along. It wasn't fair but we didn't see each other all that much anyway. Plus, we really didn't have a real committed relationship. He worked a lot on weekends and I really just saw him at school and on an occasional date. I had been told he was seeing others behind my back. I wasn't really worried about it which told me that my heart wasn't into him. I think I kept him around because I didn't want to be completely alone. Mel had Ronnie. Chase was away in Europe and Mercer had his girl of the week; Robert was too far away at school. I felt alone as it was in my life so I held onto things that sometimes were a waste of my time. When Mel and Ronnie went out alone, with Chase in Europe and Mercer at frat parties, I guess I just needed something to do and someone to spend time with.

Brad and I met on campus. He knew everything about me somehow. I would sometimes even see him on the beach near my house randomly. It seemed like we were destined to date at first with all the coincidences of running into each other. Unless, of course, he was like Amy and knew how to find me which Chase and Mercer had mentioned to me. He just "happened" to be on the beach near my house which is semi-private and not a beach most people would go to. I guess it seemed far-fetched to think it was just a coincidence but maybe he was just trying to catch my attention because he liked me. I remember one time I was in the library in the science section doing some research on echinoderms, which are basically star fish, sea urchins and sea cucumbers. There would be "no" reason whatsoever for Brad to be in that section of the library and yet he was there…

"Summer, isn't it? I think we ran into each other a few times on campus and on the beach by your house?" lied Brad.
"Yes, I remember. How are you? And, what are you doing in this part of the library? Aren't you an education major like my friend Mercer?" I asked Brad suspiciously.
"I am but I may focus on science….and kids love to learn about the ocean so I was doing a little research" Brad told me.
"Ahhh. Sound like a good idea. I know I loved that stuff as a kid. Still do obviously" I said smiling.
"Hey, you want to grab lunch? It's already 12:30p and I am starving" asked Brad with a huge smile.
"Sure" I said as we finished up our efforts in the library and headed over to the on-campus cafeteria.

That's how Brad and I got to know each other a little. It was a lunch here and there. A movie once in a while or meeting up on campus in between classes to hang out. We would start to see each other every so often on weekends when he wasn't working. We never really had a discussion that we were boyfriend and girlfriend or that we were exclusive but Brad would call me "baby" and he would say things like "it's me and you so let's not mess this up" before I would go out with friends. It was like he tried to send me out feeling guilty and to make sure I wasn't going to hook up with anyone else. It was a really strange relationship. I liked him but it wasn't like we were passionate about each other or anything. That was definitely not the case at all. We never said "I love you" or anything like that. Deep down I knew I was wasting my time with him. There was something almost dark about him. I think I was a little drawn to that in a way because I had a lot of sadness in me and misery loves company.

Brad and his best friend John were getting degrees in Education just like Mercer and were in a lot of classes with Mercer. Brad worked a lot bartending because his family had money struggles and he had a lot of student loans. It also meant he wasn't around much on weekends to hang out which allowed me to be with Mel, Ronnie, Mercer, and eventually Chase when he returned, more often. It also meant Brad was around a lot of intoxicated girls all the time too at the bar he worked at a few towns away. Mercer thought it was convenient that he didn't bartend closer and would pick a town so far away so that I wouldn't know what he was doing or who he was hanging out with. I guess I should have been more concerned but in my mind, it was what it was. If things were ever meant to be between Brad and me, it would somehow work out in the end. Plus, I secretly liked that he wasn't around much. I treasured my time with my true friends that knew me inside and out and it gave me the freedom I wanted and needed.

Chase would send me postcards almost every other week. He thought it was more fun than just texting and sending pictures and I really looked forward to them. I collected them all and put them inside my journal. He told me he missed me incredibly. I couldn't help but think that I hoped he missed me as more than a friend. I had Brad now kind of but he would never be Chase. I knew I was wasting my time but I felt like Chase was doing something with his life and I was stuck and needed to try and forge forward. I tried to keep myself busy in between the post-cards and skype calls with Chase. I would try to learn braid styles on my hair. I loved to put my long blonde hair in messy braids and I played around with make-up and skin care. I was on this whole beauty thing because I felt lonely and depressed. Feeling depressed made me feel ugly even though it was more of a feeling on the inside than the outside. I couldn't imagine being away from

Chase the entire year. It felt like an eternity. It made me appreciate him even more in my life. Even making changes, like dating, working hard in school and working, I never felt whole. Chase was spending his time going to school, studying and traveling around Europe. He told me he wasn't with anyone and just wanted to grow up and put his priorities in order. I wanted to believe him. He was always such a party boy but I wasn't sure what he meant about priorities. Did he mean focus on school and quit drinking so much? Did he mean find the right girl? He never elaborated. Chase and I could talk for hours about anything but deep down I always felt he never really told me certain things and I guess I did the same thing to him. We had known each other our whole lives so I guess it's just the way it goes.

My last conversation with Chase left me so confused. He told me that he wanted to finally be the man I needed him to be. He said he knew I had always mothered him and taken care of him and I tried to tell him that it wasn't just me doing that for him, he did it for me too. He was always there for me especially during the loss of my parents. He took care of me too and still does. I told him he was already the man I needed him to be. He just smiled and said part of him going to Europe was really for him more than me as it turned out. It was more about him feeling better about himself inside so that he could be better towards the people he cared about. I guess he too had his demons. He had everything on a silver platter since the day he was born but he was never the type to let that show. His parents raised him right and he always valued everyone and never judged anyone either. I think he liked to party a little bit too much but we were young and who didn't really? I just wondered what he was soul-searching for and I could relate because I felt the same way. Half of the time I didn't know what really bothered me. Obviously I longed for my parents and that would never change but I always felt empty too and it wasn't the emptiness from my parents. It was something else. I was just glad that junior year had flown and now it was already spring time and Chase would be coming home soon. I wondered if he would change in some way. I wondered if he missed me as much as I missed him.

School was a lot of work. So, I only worked part-time at the aquarium during the school year and full-time in the summer for the camp program when we were off for the summer. Spring breaks were fun times during school too. I guess you could say the tradition of going on vacations with the Minella family had now transitioned to going on vacations for Spring Break with the college buddies. Besides summers were so busy with the camp program, it was our only chance to get away. Junior year spring break we went to Cancun, Mexico. This would be the first time I didn't go somewhere with Chase. Mel and I decided to have a girls-only vacation and went to Cancun to live it up. Chase had just arrived back from Europe for a visit and to start bringing his stuff back. I wished I would've known he was coming back that week but Mel and I already had the plans set. He only had a few more weeks left of his abroad experience and was coming back for good thankfully. Chase was with his parents visiting Ryan at school in North Carolina. I knew he did not want to go at all but when I told him that he was lucky to have family to go visit, I guess he couldn't really argue with me on it. Besides, in just two more weeks he would be back for good permanently and I thanked God for that.

Ronnie wasn't happy either that Mel was going with me to a place full of drunken guys and was afraid they might hit on her. We were only going for a 4-day weekend and had switched our hours around at the aquarium to go so I didn't think that Ronnie should worry over a weekend long trip but I could understand his concerns. Plus, Mel and I had made arrangements to get massages and other spa-like activities and it was really about the two of us just spending some girl time together and not about hanging out and getting plastered. Besides, Mel loved Ronnie with all her heart. Their relationship reminded me of my parents. It was love at first sight and there was no turning back for them. I admired that and wished I had the same.

It was finally our Spring Break. We arrived down in Cancun early on a Thursday morning and checked into our hotel. You could tell that Cancun was a serious party town for the week with all the college students everywhere and most were wasted early in the morning already. We spent all day Thursday hanging out on the beach getting a tan. There were lots of cute guys everywhere trying to get our attention and inviting us to parties or out to clubs and bars. It was pretty comical and the attention was kind of fun. It also felt good that no one knew me, my situation or felt sorry for me. It was the break I needed. Mel and I had room service dinner and then got ready to go out on the town. We hit up a popular club there called "Carlos n Charlie's". I REALLY wanted my margarita but was really afraid to have anything with ice in it because I had heard about the water down here and how sick you could get so I stuck with beer, much to my dismay. We hung out there till about one o'clock in the morning trying to push away guys who wanted to "hook up". We met a bunch of NJ boys that were there for Spring Break and went to a school in Northern NJ and hung out with them for most of the night until we left. Mel and I got up early the next day and went to the spa for the works and it was my treat to Mel's delight. We got manicures and pedicures, a facial and a full-body massage.

"I could do this every day for the rest of my life" said Mel so relaxed.
"Me too and it's nice to just be here with you. I know we see each other all the time but it's always with the guys around or with school and work so it feels good to just do our own thing" I agreed.
"We should've gone for the whole week" said Mel.
"I know....we only have 2 nights left" I said disappointedly.

Mel and I ate lunch and then hit the pool. We worked on getting a darker tan all afternoon. We were so relaxed after our spa experience and it felt good to just relax. We left and grabbed a bite to eat before heading up for a shower and then we were meeting up with the NJ boys to just hang out at their hotel for a party instead of hitting the clubs and bars.

"Chase just texted me. He said he is having a great time at Ryan's. I am surprised to hear that.

I know he was dreading it" I said sounding somewhat stunned.
"Ronnie texted me too saying he is having a blast hanging out with Mercer"
said Mel taken aback.
"I wonder if they just want us to "think" they
are having a good time so that they
won't really show their jealousy of us being away" I said laughing.

Mel laughed too and agreed and we headed out looking really sexy and cute. Both Mel and I had on form-fitting sun-dresses and we looked quite good in my opinion. We made it to the boy's hotel a few hotels down from us and knocked on their door.

"NJ hotties are here, alright!" said one of the boys named Michael.
Mel and I laughed and said "thanks for having us".

NJ boys had a big table set up in their room and it looked like they had stolen some of the plastic chairs from down by the pool area to surround it. We were all playing chandeliers. It was a drinking game with a pitcher of beer in the middle surrounded by your individual glass of beer and you had to play quarters and get the quarter in the pitcher and then down your beer. The last person to down their beer had to drink the entire pitcher. I was anxious about playing because I knew I couldn't handle liquor and wasn't used to really drinking beer but I didn't want to not fit in and played a few rounds. Much to my dismay, I lost twice and ended up drinking the entire pitcher of beer twice too! UGH! The room was spinning now. We were there for several hours and I remember when I tried to stand up, I couldn't. Mel was pretty drunk too and really couldn't help me so a boy named Michael said he would help us get back to our hotel. Mel, Michael and I walked back or I should say "carried me back". My phone was going off like crazy and it was Chase. He wanted to know "where I was". What did he care? It wasn't like he was going to meet up with me. He was in North Carolina.

Chase was actually miserable in North Carolina. Early on Friday morning, his parents couldn't help but notice. They weren't sure if he was just being the typical "I'm too old to hang out with my parents" or if there was something else bothering him.

"What's going on Chase? You are here but your mind is not" said Abbie.
"I'm sorry. I just want to be in Cancun. I hate
Summer being there without me.
All those guys are going to swarm all over her" said Chase jealously.
Abbie couldn't help but smile and nudged her husband…
"Why don't you just go there then?" said Abbie.
"You don't mind? It would be all the way there for only
2 nights? It's just that I have been apart from her for too
long but if you don't mind?" inquired Chase.
"Just go. You were here all week. You are young. Go and have fun" said
Sam hoping Chase would finally tell Summer how he felt about her.

Chase called Ronnie and bought the two of them tickets and they met in the airport in Mexico since Chase flew from North Carolina and Ronnie flew from New Jersey. They got to Cancun late on Friday night around 8:30p. They didn't want the girls to know so they had texted them earlier about how "great" things were going without them to throw them off. They arrived at the hotel. They knew the hotel the girls were staying at but had no idea where they might be on a Friday night on an island full of party people. Summer wasn't answering his texts and he just prayed they would find them soon since they didn't even have anywhere to stay.

Ronnie and Chase found out the room they were in from the front desk and waited outside the girl's room for a while taking turns going to the lobby to look around for them too. The girls were obviously out for the night so they went by the pool and hung out at the bar there ordering drinks. It was close to midnight when Chase could see Summer, Mel and some guy with his arm around Summer. His blood boiled. He hated Summer being here with no one to protect her. He hadn't seen her all year while he got his act together and being away was what he needed to make sure his feelings were true. Chase figured that he needed to be on his own and away from his sheltered and wealthy life. He needed to go somewhere no one knew him. Where he could meet people on his own terms, find out what he really wanted in life and be put in situations with women to see how he would want to act. His feelings it turned out were truer than true for Summer and the truth is being away in Europe only made him realize how much in love he was with Summer. She was the future he wanted for no reason other than being her.

Ronnie and Chase walked behind them and then would sneak up on them.

> *"Thanks for walking us back Michael. As you can tell I am not used to drinking" I said thanking him.*
> *"No problem. Listen…if you ever want to hang out back in NJ too, here is my number" said Michael handing me his phone number.*
> *"She already has a boyfriend" said Chase from behind them.*

Mel and I turned around to see the two boys.

> *"Oh my God!" screamed Mel and ran to hug Ronnie. Chase came over and sort of pushed Michael out of the way and seeing I was drunk picked me up and said "I'll take her from here. See ya".*

I felt bad as Michael walked away like a sad puppy dog. He was only being nice but I was glad to see Chase.

> *"I am so glad you are here" I said and gave him a squeeze and a kiss on the cheek while he carried me to the room.*
> *"Are you?" sneered Chase.*

*"Yes, I am. You know I can't handle drinking
and I got pressured into it" I told him.
"It was the only time I got drunk. I swear. We went
to the spa and ordered room service and
just hung out swimming and tanning" I told Chase.*

I never knew why I felt like I needed to explain myself but I always felt that way with him. He had a hold on me for some reason and I never wanted him to think I would do something he would disapprove of, even though, he constantly did things I disapproved of.

*"I really am glad you surprised us Chase. I secretly wanted you here.
I hate going away without you and I have missed
you so so much" I confided to Chase.*
*"Me too" Chase agreed. "I felt like something was missing the whole
week being back in the States without having you around."*
"Did you guys plan this the entire time?" Mel asked Ronnie.
*"No, I didn't have the money to but would've
done it on my own if I could afford it.
It was Chase. I don't think he liked Summer being down here without him
around to be her body guard. You know how
the two of them are" said Ronnie.*
*"I don't know why they just don't get together
and get it over with" laughed Mel.*

Our last Saturday, we all had a blast swimming, eating and drinking (except for me on the drinking part after last night)! We went out to Carlos n Charlie's again Saturday night and had a blast. NJ boys were there too and they hung out with all of us too for a while. Chase was nicer to them now and we all were dancing and having a good time. We all flew out together on Sunday and headed back to Avon-by-the-Sea. It was a great trip overall. I was exhausted but for good reasons for once. It was a blast. I had to be at work Monday morning early at the aquarium and it always felt good to get back home. Just a few more weeks and the summer camp program at the aquarium would begin so we were trying to organize and get everything ready for the kids.

Summertime was finally here. Chase was back thankfully and that made me really happy. Every summer through school, I worked the summer camp program that I had grown up going to at the aquarium. Chase was working for a local accounting firm this summer to gain experience for his degree in Finance. Mel, Ronnie and I did a great job with the camp. The kids were exposed to science experiments, crafts, nature-led programs, animal anatomy, marine mammals and how we are all connected to the ocean. We did a lot of things outside the aquarium and even rented a bus to go down to Cape May to visit Ron Johnson's foundation to help the kids learn more about how they could give back to the environment and the beaches. I knew Chase missed the aquarium too. He liked the accounting and finance stuff but he loved the beaches and marine life too. He came to visit me often for lunch since he was just a few blocks away working for a local CPA. Just yesterday, he came on his lunch break to teach the kids about Marine Mammals. This was my favorite subject in Marine Biology as I loved animals so very much.

Chase brought stuffed animals of five different animals. He had a seal, a dolphin, a sea otter, a manatee and a polar bear. He taught them about the five groups of marine mammals and how each stuffed animal he brought fit into one of those categories. I shared how marine mammals are like other mammals but they have adapted to living all or part of their life in the ocean. The learning session went over really well with the kids and those who asked questions got to keep a stuffed animal, which of course they loved. I brought dolphin key chains too for the kids who didn't get a stuffed animal. Working around kids as much as I do, I knew there would be some tears if they didn't at least get something.

My favorite day of the summer program with the kids is the day we have an outing at the beach with the kids called "Beach Treasure". They were tasked with finding five items to bring back to discuss at lunch time. It could be shells, shark teeth, drift wood, pretty much anything. Then, over lunch, we would discuss their findings. Mel made sure to tell them to bring back garbage too. She wanted the kids to know that people are the number one cause of why the beaches have become the way they are and that we need to remember to do our part to not litter and clean up after others sometimes too when necessary. Chase and I had done this exact project when we were kids at the camp. We were always trying to out-do each other with our findings. Somehow, he always won and it drove me crazy. He could always seem to find anything especially shark teeth and those were nearly impossible to find. Yet, he wasn't able to find my SUMMER necklace. Go figure.

I always looked forward to this camp activity. It was a beautiful, sunny day on the beach. I had a good feeling about the day and today was going to turn out to be a memorable day for me. I was slowly starting to remember how to feel myself again…not completely but I felt little pieces of my personality coming back and was feeling good on this particular day. There was a little girl in this year's camp program named Jennie. She had her hair in blonde braids every day and was tiny like I always was. She was a mini-me. Chase had come and met me for lunch earlier in the week and said she could have been my daughter. He said he wanted to come back later in the week again for lunch but it was already Friday and he seemed too busy at work to escape. Mel, Ronnie and I watched as the kids were running around like crazy all morning finding the treasures of the beach and waters. I couldn't wait to see what they had come up with. Not Jennie though…she was already done she told me and gave me a wink. I could tell she was excited to share her findings. She was acting very secretive and suspicious. It was noon now so Ronnie called all the kids back and we had set up blankets on the sand and we were getting ready for our picnic lunch. I loved to relax and eat on the beach, even when you got the sand in your sandwich which always seemed to happen whether there is wind or not. We passed out their lunch boxes and handed out juice boxes.

"OK, listen up everyone. We are going to get ready to share your amazing findings" shouted Mel.

One by one the kids went around and shared their findings which included a star fish, a variety of shells and rocks, a fish, a sand crab and a variety of other treasures. All of the kids were so proud. It was so fun to watch their excited faces light up as they shared their treasures. It was Jennie's turn to talk about the items she had found. She hid them behind her back and was very secretive and giggly during the whole morning. I knew she had something special to share but couldn't figure out what it was. One by one, she put four flowers on the blanket. All four were pink roses, my favorite.

"I can't believe you found those" I told her.
"I have one more thing that I found on the beach" Jennie said excitedly since she so far only had four items and she pointed over to a blanket of sunbathers sitting nearby.

Looking over, I saw it was Chase! He came over holding 8 more pink roses to make a dozen.

"These are for you, Summer" said Chase "except for this one"
and he handed one to Jennie who gave him a hug.
"I can't believe you are here! You surprised me. Thank you so much. This is why I love you!"
I said and hugged him. All of the kids laughed and a few said "yuck"
as Chase and I laughed. Jennie asked "is Chase your boyfriend?"

Chase told the kids we were "secret boyfriend/girlfriend". I have no idea what that meant but the kids loved it! Chase was always good with kids. I wondered why he had picked such a stuffy degree when his heart always seemed to be in the same place as mine. Maybe he just loved math too. I wasn't sure.

> "I have to run" said Chase, "I just wanted to surprise you and have fun with the kids, especially Jennie. I remember doing this when we were kids. It brings back such good memories". "It does" I said, "Thank you so much for the flowers. They are my favorite". "I know" said Chase, "I'll call you later" he said walking off the beach towards his truck.

Mel walked over by me as Chase walked away.

> "What was that all about? Hmmmm??" said Mel.
> "Shut up! He was just being sweet Mel" I told her.

We went back over to the kids and were starting to pack them up to head back up to the aquarium.

> "Summer and Chase...sitting in a tree, K-I-S-S-I-N-G!" teased Ronnie. "I am going to kill you" I joked and jumped on Ronnie's back as if I could ever tackle him while Mel laughed.

The kids of course loved it. I don't know why Chase did it but it made my whole summer that year. He knew summer was my favorite season with the beaches, surfing, warm weather, my birthday but it was also a hard time for me with the loss of my parents on that fateful 4th of July. He just knew me and wanted me to have something nice to focus on I kept trying to convince myself. You couldn't erase the smile off my face for once and it hadn't been seen in a while.

It's true that Chase probably knew me better than anyone. He knew me when my parents were alive, he knew me when we had diapers on, and he knew me from sleeping with me at night to comfort me after my parents died. He had seen me in my underwear, a bikini and one time, he claims, naked. Although, I always tell him that must have been a dream! He knew that I loved pink roses. My mom loved flowers and always had fresh flowers in our kitchen sitting on the island. Most of the time, they were roses and when they were pink ones, I always said they were my favorite. Chase heard me say it so many times that he would see them and say "I know – those are your favorite". I guess he still remembered. Once we got back inside the aquarium, I stopped by my office and I pulled out my journal from my bag and looked at the picture from my parents wedding day where my mom was holding the pink roses and I held mine as I stared at it. It made me smile. My mom and I were so happy in those moments and it was nice to share it with her even if it was in a far-fetched way.

CHAPTER 6

Surfing and Summer

It was still the summer before our senior year in college and Mercer was busy typing away on his blog. He had to create an educational blog for one of his summer classes as a part of his teaching experience. It didn't surprise me one bit that his blog was an educational guide to surfing. Who would've thought any different? He was putting together the basics of the blog….a guide to surf equipment and essentials, weather conditions, types of boards, waves, locations to surf and the reasons why, etc. I told him to make sure he has a section on safety. There are always beginners out there, which is great but they don't know the lay of the land and can cause injuries. It's all about respect to the locals. They drop in on a wave or let go of their surfboards or do other things that can cause themselves or others injury. I could tell this was becoming my project too as Mercer wrote down every word I said. I also suggested having a "local surfer of the month" page that highlighted one of the locals and told a little bit about them as well as links to local surf stores and lessons might be helpful too.

I have never seen someone so excited about school work before in my life. Mercer had hired a photographer to come and photograph him as well as Chase and me surfing all afternoon so that he could download the pictures onto the blog for the different sections. We also gathered all our boards and borrowed some from the surf shop that Mercer worked at that were used for rentals so that we could photograph the different types of boards to help with the education of buying your first board part of the blog. I couldn't wait to see how the blog turned out. I told Mercer that I thought this was going to be something he would end up maintaining after the project ended because it sounded incredible. It was such a great afternoon hanging at the beach, surfing and getting our pictures taken. I couldn't imagine a more perfect day. It was good practice too because there was a surfing competition coming up and we were all entered in it. I was so happy Chase was back from Europe and we could do something fun together.

They were having the North East Regional Surfing Competition in Avon-by-the-Sea this summer and the whole town was excited. They had long board, body board and open surfing competitors from all over the North East area coming to compete by age group. It meant a lot of business for the town. As a part of the contest, there was also a large seafood festival on the boardwalk across my house as well as vendors, parades and other events. I know Mel's parents were excited to have the extra business at their donut shop in town. It was an annual event. I entered often as a kid but hadn't done it in a few years and wanted to give it a try again. I had been surfing daily with Chase and Mercer so we were at the height of our skills. They had one special contest too for best local surfer talent also categorized by age - boy (12-14 and 15-17), girl (14 and under), men (18-24 and 25+) and women (18-24 and 25+) categories. Chase and Mercer were entering the men 18-24 category and I decided to enter the women 18-24 category too. The prize was being featured in an ad in one of the sponsor's wet suit catalogs, a voucher for a custom surf board, $2,500, a trophy, and of course, bragging rights. We were just doing it for fun more than the prizes but we were all super-competitive too so the outcome should be very interesting especially between Mercer and Chase. Mercer said he would feature all of the winners as his very first "local surfers of the month" that I had suggested on his blog too. Despite the local aspect, most people here were not even from the North East. Traveling pros from Brazil, Australia and Costa Rica among others came as well. Avon-by-the-Sea had a great history of waves and the event drew people from all over who would get a chance to meet the pros in person and see them surf live.

This coming Saturday was the competition so we were supposed to be hanging low on Friday night to rest up before the event. We had spent the whole day at my house bringing food back from the seafood festival and having a few drinks here and there too. Mel and I had shopped the various vendors and found some cute bracelets. It was evening now and of course, Mercer and Chase chose to still party and not get any rest. We were going to Chase's house because his parents were away for the weekend visiting Ryan who was away at college and currently living out of State. There was a bunch of people here that Chase probably barely knew but ever the social butterfly had invited. Most of them were local surfers or other people here for the contest. Brad was here too. We had been dating briefly on and off and he showed up with his buddy John much to Mercer's dismay. Brad and his friend John were hanging out with some girls that they seemed to know from North Jersey that were down the shore for the event. There were a few guys from New York City that had taken an interest in me and were trying to convince me to drink.

"C'mon Summer. Do some shots with us?" said the NYC boys.
"No way! You'll be wishing you hadn't when
I win tomorrow and you go home
without a prize" I told them laughing.
Mercer came up and enthusiastically said "I'll do one Dudes".
"Mercer, you are already drunk, aren't you?" I said.

One of the NYC surfers named Parker seemed particularly interested in me. He reminded me a lot of Chase in terms of looks. He had dirty blonde hair that was almost shaggy in style with long bangs with an almost a razor-like appearance around his ears and neck. I knew the girls probably swooned over him. He had light blue eyes too, very similar to mine. Parker came over and sat next to me. I couldn't help but notice how handsome he was. He had the perfect, ripped body and he wore his button up Billabong white shirt with almost all the buttons undone exposing his chest. He had on a choker type necklace made of white shells with black and brown coconut beads. I always had a thing for the surfer type I couldn't help but think. Too bad Brad was here watching my every move in between flirting with his slew of girls from North Jersey. I had a feeling he was probably cheating on me with at least one of them based on the dirty looks they would send my way every so often. I wondered what he told them about me. I didn't really care anyway sadly.

"Summer, right?" inquired Parker.
"Yes. Parker, correct?" I replied.
"Yes. So tell me about yourself. You are absolutely beautiful by the way. I apologize if I kept staring at you. There are definitely no girls around where I am in Manhattan that look anything like you do" said Parker complimenting me. "Other than really not a drinker and beautiful, tell me about you".
I kind of blushed when I replied. He was so charming and cute. This is the type of guy you could get lost in. I needed to dump Brad and find someone who I had more in common with I couldn't help but think.
"Well, I live practically across the street in the blue house" I said pointing down Ocean Avenue "and I am about to be a senior at Monmouth University majoring in Marine Biology. I am an only child and as you can see I love to surf and love anything pretty much having to do with the ocean."
"I go to Fordham University. I am pre-med there. I went to high school in New York City but I am actually from Santa Monica, California" shared Parker as I couldn't help but think he looked like the absolute definition of the perfect California dream boy.
"I grew up surfing so moving to NY as a freshman in high school kind of sucked from that perspective but my dad got relocated there for work

*so no choice really but I try to surf whenever I can. School obviously is pretty intense being pre-med so I don't have a lot of time and never really get out of the Bronx where my school is located" finished Parker.
"Pre-med. Wow. Any focus on what type of medicine yet?" I asked.
"Yes, pediatric cancer. I lost a younger sister to cancer so I kind of made it my lifetime commitment to help children with cancer and assist in research to find cures" shared Parker.
"That's amazing Parker. I am really into Marine Biology because the oceans too were always so important to my father and he grew up here. So I guess in a way we are doing similar things" I told him without going into the whole "my parents are not here anymore" story.
"So, do you have a boyfriend? Not putting you on the spot but wanted to ask. I'll be honest, I have been with the same girl since high school but she goes to school at University of Central Florida so we are apart more than we are together and for example, she didn't even come home this summer" Parker told me.
"I have been seeing Brad who is here tonight but I wouldn't exactly call him my boyfriend. Honestly, I think I just haven't found the right person yet" I confided to him.*

Brad had now come up and pulled me onto his lap as Chase walked over and gave me a look of disappointment. He hated Brad too but I think it was more about me talking to Parker than Brad that irritated him. Brad obviously only came over because I was talking to Parker too. He could do whatever he wanted but I wasn't allowed to talk to anyone.

*"I am not drunk yet so I'll take that shot if you don't mind" said Chase.
"Chase, stop drinking. I know you want to beat Mercer, don't you?" I said trying to convince him to stop drinking with the motivation of beating Mercer.
"Why don't you go back to your gang of boys that you have by the balls?" he nastily replied in front of everyone.*

*"Chase, what are you talking about?" I asked
kind of shocked at his strong words as I
left Brad and Parker to approach him.
"Please, they are drooling over you Summer and
you are loving it" snapped Chase.
"Oh my God...I haven't done anything. You really should stop drinking.
It's obviously affecting your perception" I snapped back.
"Whatever Summer" shouted Chase.*

Chase was obviously drunk.....a bad move with the competition tomorrow. He actually almost tripped and fell when he was walking away from me. It was close to midnight now and most people were heading out since the competition started at 8:00 a.m. in the morning. I figured I would stay and clean up a little for Chase even though he had "people" that would probably do it. I didn't want the house to be a disaster or have his parent's find out. I couldn't find Chase anywhere.

*"Mercer, have you seen Chase? " I inquired.
"No, babe" replied Mercer and he gave me a hug as he was also going to
head out..."see you in the a.m.".*

Oh well, I thought I better go or I won't be up to par tomorrow. Brad and John were going with the "North Jersey" girls to some club so I said good-bye to Brad. Parker and his friends seemed to linger until Brad left and I couldn't help but hope that Parker was waiting to talk more to me. I went up to Chase's bedroom to grab my purse real quick and walked in on him and, yuck, Amy! I had been so preoccupied talking to Parker, I didn't even realize Amy was there.

*"I am so sorry. I didn't think anyone was in here...
I....I... just wanted my purse" I stuttered.
"Obviously someone is in here and it is MY bedroom" snapped Chase in
one of the nastiest moods I had seen him in for a while.*

*"I'm sorry" was all I could say and I grabbed my purse
and ran down the stairs and out the door where I saw
Parker and his friends about to get in their car.
"Bye guys" I yelled over. Parker left them really quickly
and came up to me and gave me a hug.
"I really liked talking to you Summer" he said
while slipping me a piece of paper.
"It's my cell phone number. I know we don't live really close but
it's not that far so if you want to go out some time or just even
start talking or whatever, call me or text me so that I have your
number too and then we'll see what happens" said Parker.
"That would be great. Thanks and good luck tomorrow. Hopefully I
will see you" I said as he ran back to the car to head to their hotel.*

So, Chase was hooking up with psycho Amy. This is why she remained the stalker...he always led her on. But, I guess he liked her if they were getting it on in his bedroom. It really pissed me off and his attitude sucked. I left and went home by myself. Brad was off with his so called friends and Chase was obviously busy. I really liked talking to Parker. Realistically though, he was pre-med and living outside of Manhattan at Fordham. It didn't seem realistic that we could have a good chance at getting to know each other when he was so busy and kind of far. Plus, he had a girlfriend. As soon as I got home, I put his number into the contacts in my phone. I wasn't sure if I would ever call or text him to give him my number but I put it in there just in case. I quickly washed my face and brushed my teeth and threw on a nightgown and slid into bed. I wanted to get a good night's sleep. At around two o'clock in the morning I heard someone jiggling at my apartment door. At first I thought someone better not be trying to break in but then I also thought I hoped it wasn't Brad...I wasn't in the mood to be bothered and it really pissed me off because he knew I wanted to kick butt tomorrow. I heard someone start to knock and I yelled "who is it" as I grabbed a baseball bat that I kept next to my bed anyway living alone.

"I'm sorry Summer. I'm sorry" the voice slurred.

I would recognize that voice anywhere. It was Chase... He was even too drunk to remember where I hid my key I couldn't help but think.

"What are you doing Chase? I was sleeping. Tomorrow is the competition" I told him concerned.
"I just love you Summer and I am sorry. I was mean but you were really all over those guys tonight and acting crazy" he slurred obviously wasted out of his mind.
"Do you like Parker? Did you hook up with him? I saw you guys talking and I could tell he likes you. Tell me and look me in the eyes when you do it!"

I knew I hadn't done anything at all and was all over no one so I just told him to come and lay down next to me and go to sleep. There was no arguing with a drunken guy. Chase climbed in to my bed and I told him nothing happened with Parker and to just go to sleep and he cuddled with me and passed out. I reached over and set my alarm clock for even earlier now that I would have to sober him up in the morning. Fun stuff.... But I was glad to have him back and sleeping in my bed with me again. I had missed this so much but not really when he is wasted and passed out but I still was happy he was here with me.

My alarm clock went off at 7:00 a.m. It didn't even stir Chase and I couldn't help but think I had pretty much not slept at all. The competition started at 8:00 a.m. and I had hoped to go there the whole day to watch the different events, meet some of the pros and hang out but it wasn't looking like that was going to be possible with Chase passed out cold next to me. I didn't have to compete till 11:00 a.m. but had to register by 10:00 a.m. so I figured worst case scenario I would be there by 9:30 a.m. or 10:00 a.m. Chase was going at 1:00 p.m. but had to be there by 10:00 a.m. to register too. I slid carefully and quietly out of bed since Chase was practically smothering me.

He held on so tight to me last night that I couldn't breathe. I put on a pot of coffee and hopped into the shower. I walked back into my bedroom and looked over at Chase.

> "Chase? You have to get up soon. It's almost
> 8:00 a.m. and you need to sober up"
> I told him while I shook him a little.
> "I can't get up. I need ten more minutes" he said looking
> at me and then lifting his head…."Are you naked?"
> "I just got out of the shower so obviously I have no
> clothes on under my towel pervert" I said to him.

I grabbed my bathing suit and rash guard and put it on in the bathroom and finished getting ready. Then, I pulled Chase out of bed and into the bathroom and made him take a shower. While he was in the shower, I went out into the kitchen and made breakfast – just toast and coffee for Chase. I had a banana and orange juice with my toast. I wanted to have energy for the competition and I was going to compete before Chase was. Chase came out and we ate breakfast. I could tell he was hurting. I didn't even bring up last night. I was an avoider and so was he. Mercer called Chase asking where he was. He was already down at the event, where I wanted to be already too! We finished up breakfast and I grabbed my bag and my board and we walked over to Chase's house to grab his stuff too and then headed down to the beach to sign up for the event by registration deadline. We made it just in time at 9:50 a.m. I had only an hour before I was on…

New York City surfer guys were there but no Brad yet. I wondered if he would show or be too wasted. He was always missing when I needed someone to support me. Mel and Ronnie came up with Stella to watch me. Now it was sinking in and I was starting to get a little nervous. I surfed for the love of it not really the competition of it but I had signed up for this now and there was no turning back.

"You are going to kick butt Summer" said Mel
supportively and giving me a hug.
"Good luck" said Ronnie and he hugged me too.
*"Just have fun. I know you will be good but just
have fun"* said Stella the eternal optimist.

Mercer and Chase walked up too to wish me good luck.

"Kill the wave Summer" said Mercer and Chase
just simply gave me a kiss on the cheek and
said "good luck".

Chase was definitely hurting. I told him not to drink. I yawned as I was stretching and getting ready.

*"Why are you so tired Summer? I thought you went
to bed early last night, no?"* asked Mel
"I did". I don't know why I lied.

Chase overheard and sort of looked down and walked off to sit down on a towel with Ronnie and Mercer. I knew he probably felt bad for waking me up last night although it would have been nice to hear it from him. I wanted to be on my best game and it's hard with just a few hours of sleep. Parker waved at me and gave me a thumbs up.

There were six women in my age group and I knew all of them. They were from Avon-by-the-Sea and all were actually a year or two older than me except for one – Mary Lovent. She was two years younger and a pretty talented surfer so I knew I had to catch the best wave there was. One by one the girls went…you only got one shot. It was a little bit of luck and a lot of skill. The ocean was pretty rough today and the waves were probably head-high. You had to be a good surfer. I pulled off my rash guard and threw on my spring suit wet suit. The water was pretty cold today for some reason and I wanted to keep up my stamina. I wanted to make sure I picked a pretty heavy wave. The bigger the wave is…the better for me. The fourth girl was up now and did a decent ride. I was next and then Mary. At least I didn't have to follow her in case she did awesome and it would just make me feel more pressured. I ducked under the wave and made it out sitting on my board waiting for that perfect moment.

    I could see all of the people watching from the shore and my heart was racing. I tried to find a thought in my mind that would help me ignore them and concentrate. I thought about Mercer. He was such an awesome surfer and I remembered in high school one time, he was just being crazy and decided to surf naked. He was "hanging eleven" if you know what I mean. I smiled and that memory helped me forget that there were hundreds of people on the beach watching and waiting. I could see the wave I wanted to catch getting ready to go and paddled hard to get to it. I was paddling harder than I normally needed to because I was exhausted from the night before but there was no way that was going to hold me back. I made it and stood on deck and held my own. The ocean was really a gift and I knew to value and respect it. I always felt a connection with it and thought of my dad as I eased through the wave. I did a frontside cutback using the rail of my board to gain speed and it thrilled the crowd. Finally, I made it to the shore. Everyone clapped for me and I had a blast. My friends came over and hugged me and we just sort of waited as Mary made her way. She was sitting out there for a while. I guess she was feeling the same way I did and didn't want to go last. It was a hard spot to be in.

    Parker came up and hugged me too and then ran back up by his friends to walk up to the seafood festival for lunch before they went on this afternoon. I guess he had come to watch me I couldn't help but think feeling flattered. Chase overheard Parker and his friends talking as they gathered up their stuff to head up to grab food. All of them were saying how hot Summer was. With her long blonde hair, blue eyes and smoking body, especially her chest. He was angry inside because he was jealous but he also had to agree. Summer was the most beautiful girl in the world. He hoped Summer didn't ever get into anything with Parker. He wasn't sure he could compete with him. He walked over by Summer, Mel, Mercer and Ronnie to watch Mary surf.

We all yelled to support Mary. As much as I wanted to win, she was a local surfer and we always had each other's backs. I could see Mary paddling in and she caught a pretty nice wave. She rode it smooth and well. She had perfect form and balance. Now, it was just up to the judges.... There would be only one winner since this was just a side-bar competition for the local community. The boys and girls categories were already done and it was just this category and then the men's groups left. I could see one of the judges walking up to the microphone with the paper. Please let it be me was all I could think but if anyone else, Mary. She did really well too.

> "Thank you girls for a job well done...there can only
> be one winner and the best local surfer and
> winner of the $2500, an advertisement in a
> national wet suit campaign and of course
> our one-of-a-kind championship trophy goes to.... *Summer Wright*".

I went up and accepted my award and everyone hugged me. It was an awesome feeling. Everything my dad had taught me about the ocean and respecting it helped me surf so much better. In a way, I owed this to him (not that picturing Mercer naked surfing didn't help). I looked around and couldn't help but notice that Brad didn't show up. He really let me down. If he was involved in something, I would've been there to support him. He was a crappy boyfriend. Mercer and Chase were up now. Mel, Ronnie, Stella and I grabbed food and sat on Stella's blanket to watch them.

> "This should be interesting" said Mel.
> "I know...Mercer versus Chase. If Chase wins, he will be
> thrilled to finally beat Mercer at surfing. If Mercer wins, it's
> just another notch on his belt" said Ronnie with a smile.

> *"Chase was such a mess last night. I hope he didn't
> do himself in because of it" I said worried.*

Mercer was going first and Chase was going last. At least Chase would have a little longer to get his energy, I thought. Mercer caught the frontside wave and was riding down the line like a pro. Sometimes I wondered why he didn't try and go pro. He was an amazing surfer. He started to do a bottom turn and gained speed and finished out the ride. He did it with speed and agility. It was a perfect performance and he had certainly set the bar. The other players were up and it was nothing great to mention. No one could really compete with Mercer. Probably not even Chase although there were times when Chase could be pretty equal in his tricks and moves. Chase was up now. I watched him as he walked towards the ocean with his board and couldn't help but think of how cute he is. He could be so immature though. I guess he could just make mistakes and be who he is with me because we have known each other forever. I smiled as I watched and I could see him sitting out there and he looked better so I was hoping he had his energy back. Chase paddled out and caught a decent wave. Chase was able to do a frontside cutback and was able to really get back to the source of the wave and gained a ton of speed. I watched nervously and he looked good but I could tell he didn't have the same grace as Mercer. The alcohol was showing but he did have a good ride. It was up to the judges now because they were the ones that counted….

> *"Thanks everyone. This is our men's 18-24 event
> for the local surfer competition portion
> of this weekend's event. The winner for this age group and the winner of the
> $2,500, trophy and wetsuit advertisement is…..
> drum roll…..Mercer Matthews".*

No one was really surprised and he deserved it. Stella said congratulations and headed back up to the house to check on her doggies.

Mel, Ronnie and I ran over to the boys and gave them both a hug. Chase took it well. He knew he probably could never beat Mercer anyway.

"I guess we will be modeling together Summer.
Modeling buddies" said Mercer.
"Yes, we'll show real models how to do it" I joked.

We both got our $2,500 checks. I knew exactly what I was going to do with mine. I would donate it to the conservation of the beaches in our community. I didn't need the money and I knew my parents would want me to do something like that too. I think Mel wanted me to donate it to her purse but she knew if she wanted to something, I would buy it for her. I was proudest of my trophy to be honest. It was cool to be the #1 woman local surfer even in a small town.

"I am going to go home and take a nap. I am really tired" Chase told me.
"I'll walk up with you. I am going home to take
a shower and change" I responded.
"I'll call you guys later with plans for tonight" said Mercer excitedly.

Mel and Ronnie stayed to watch some more events with Stella once she came back from letting the dogs out as Chase and I walked up the beach towards the boardwalk and then to our houses. I could see Brad's car in front of my house and he was sitting on the steps.

"Looks like you have company" said Chase.
"Yeah...I see that. He couldn't make it to see the
event though could he?" I told Chase.
"He's an idiot. Sorry about last night Summer" Chase apologized finally.
"It's o.k. Chase. You know I am here for you. I'm glad you came over.
Let me go deal with Brad and I'll text you later"
I said as I ran up towards my house.

I approached my house and walked towards Brad who was still sitting on my stairs that go up the apartment. He was holding a bouquet of various wild flowers that he probably got at the grocery store.

"Baby, you won!!! YAY! I knew you could do it"
he said smiling and hugging me carefully
so that I didn't get him all salty and wet.
"Where were you?" I said kind of standoffish.
"Sorry baby. I was just really trashed last night
and I overslept and I hurried as fast as
I could but I just got here about 10 minutes ago. You forgive me?"
asked Brad trying to sound sincere.
"I guess. Thanks for the flowers. It would've
been nice if you would have showed up
though to support me" I told him and I meant it.
"I know. I will make it up to you" said Brad trying to win me over.
"Are you coming in to hang?" I inquired.
"No, I have to be at work at 4:00 p.m. and
should be finished around 1:00 a.m.
I'll call you later though and see what you guys are up
to and try and meet up with you" Brad told me.

It was fine with me. I was kind of pissed at him for no-showing today and putting drinking and partying before me and something going on in my life that was important. Oh well. I went inside and put my trophy in my room. I took the flowers Brad gave me and stuck them in a vase and put them on the kitchen table. I couldn't help but think he could've at least gotten me my favorite flowers – pink roses. That was the thing with Brad…he never did what I hoped he would. I stopped over Stella's and gave her the check to give to my financial advisor to donate to the town to catch her before she headed back down to meet up with Mel and Ronnie. Then, I went back in and made myself a bubble bath and relaxed for about an hour or so. I wondered what Chase was doing and how he was feeling from his hangover. I felt bad that he didn't win too. I texted him a smiley face while I sat soaking in the tub – "☺". He texted back a wink – ";)". I smiled and put the phone down but then picked it back up again and stared at Parker's number in my contacts. I thought for a brief moment I should text him and see how he did with the competition. I hadn't even stayed to see his event. He came to see me so I felt kind of bad. I wondered if he would look to see if I came or not. I guess it was kind of shitty of me that I didn't go see him after he came to watch me. I wasn't sure why I didn't go. Maybe I was too tired from last night or maybe deep down I knew the relationship would take a lot of effort and I wasn't willing to give it. I wasn't sure. I did think he was pretty perfect so I don't really know why I didn't at least text him and see how things went today and keep in touch. I just lay my phone back down and didn't do it. I guess I really didn't know him that well so I thought just forget about it. As I got out of the tub, I saw Chase's watch on my sink. He must have left it there from when he took a shower here this morning. I picked it up and smiled. I liked having a little piece of Chase at my apartment.

Two weeks later, Mercer and I had our photo shoot for the wet suit catalog on the beach right near our houses. Chase watched the shoot from his balcony with his binoculars thinking that could've been him if he wasn't such an idiot. The photographer came up and explained what he was going for in the shoot. There were other winners there too but no Parker so I assumed he didn't win his category which deep down I was kind of glad because I was embarrassed that I never reached out to him to at least see what the outcome was from the event.

> "Mercer and Summer, you need to act like a couple since that is the "theme" of your portion of the shoot and we are going to do a lot of shots with you looking into each other's eyes, hugging or touching each other" advised the photographer as Mercer and I started giggling like school children.

It irritated Chase to watch although he knew Mercer would never go for Summer but it really irked him to see the two of them all over each other out there. Mercer and I had a blast. It was all really comical in a lot of ways because as much as Mercer and I cared about each other, we would never be more than friends and the thought of it and having to act like it made it really funny and it was hard not to laugh during the shoot. Truth is I wasn't Mercer's type. Mercer liked long brown hair on girls. I had long blonde hair. He also liked girls that had curves and I was too tiny for him. Hair color didn't matter for me. Looks were important of course but I liked all different kinds of people. I considered Mercer a great catch but I think there just wasn't an attraction there in that way for us and we both knew that. We didn't care anyway and were just sort of going for it for the camera.

Mercer noticed Chase watching from his balcony. He knew Chase probably wanted to be out here with Summer. He just couldn't figure out why Chase just didn't realize he had stronger feelings for Summer than he would admit to himself. Mercer put his hands through Summer's hair as they looked at each other and the camera snapped. They leaned in a little towards each other as if they were going to kiss but it was just for the camera. The photographer let them take a break and Mercer checked his phone. There was a text from Chase…"do you have to be all over Summer?" Mercer texted back… "someone should since you aren't man enough to do it". He knew it was sarcastic but Chase was pissing him off. No one could ever touch Summer and it pissed Mercer off that his best friend was second guessing his intentions. He let it go though. He wasn't going to let "jealous boy" ruin his day. That wasn't Mercer's laid-back style anyway.

Chase's dad, Sam, came out onto the balcony by him. He looked down and saw the photo shoot happening with Summer and Mercer.

"What's going on Chase? Why do you look so angry?" Sam asked concerned.
"It's nothing" lied Chase.

"Is it Summer? Tell me the truth" Sam inquired
although he already knew in his heart.
"Yes" was all Chase could say.
*"Just a word of advice son…if you love Summer, you
better do something about it before you lose her.
It's something you really need to think about. Someone
is going to snatch her up and love her.
If you love her like I think you do, you have to have
the courage to tell her"* Sam said his two cents.
"I will" said Chase not sharing much *"There is also the Brad Situation
but mostly I just have to get the courage to do it".*
"Don't wait too long Chase" advised Sam.
*"You already have been taught that
life is short when we lost Edward and Carissa. I
know Summer has been though a lot but
if she loves you like you love her, you may be pleasantly surprised
and things will only be better for both of you".*
"I know dad. I just… can't bear to lose Summer" said Chase.
"Then do something about it" encouraged Sam.

Chase was so afraid that Summer would think of him only as a friend or that he was pursuing her because of her parents' death like he was there to protect her. It couldn't be farther from the truth. Chase had always loved Summer. He was just to chicken to tell her. He didn't want to ruin what they had. Plus, Chase knew in his heart he went through a period of immaturity in high school and college. He would've hurt her and he couldn't ever do that to Summer. He had gone abroad to get his life in order. Being away from everyone put everything into perspective for him. He just didn't count on the fact that Summer would start dating someone while he was away. Chase knew that he shouldn't expect anything different though given his actions. She won't be single forever. He never told Summer the truth about how he felt. He couldn't expect her to just sit around and wait for him forever. He wasn't super worried about Brad because he knew deep down Summer probably knew it wasn't going anywhere and just strung him along. Seeing Summer talk to Parker though sparked something different in him. He knew that a great guy like Parker would be interested in Summer and steal her heart. He couldn't block every guy that Summer came across forever. His dad was right. He would end up losing her and someone would scoop her up and love her. He would be too late to do anything about it if that happened.

The photo shoot was wrapping up. I couldn't wait to see the photos they would pick from the shoot. It was such a cool experience. The other winners were there too from the local contest age levels but thankfully none of the New York City boys. The photographer agreed to take a group shot for Mercer's blog for the local surfers of the month page. Mercer interviewed each person too to put some highlights of each person on his page. We had a terrific afternoon and it was fun to pretend to be a model for a day. I would never be tall enough to be a real model. The wet suit company let us pick a wet suit to keep and gave us some other products too from their product line. We got several types of wax, lip balms, a gift card for a custom surfboard. It was amazing!!! I should enter these contests more often I thought and Mercer agreed.

"Did you see Chase watching from his house?" Mercer asked me.
"No. Do you think he wanted to be out here?" I asked Mercer.
"Yes, Summer. I do. I think he wanted to be
out here with YOU" Mercer told me.
"What do you mean Mercer?" I asked.
"I just think Chase doesn't like you with anyone but him. That's all I mean" said Mercer as he started to change the subject so that he didn't go too far and have Chase get mad at him.
"Custom surfboard – cool, huh?" Mercer smiled.
"Oh my God, yes! I cannot wait and I know exactly what I am going to get" I told him happily.

CHAPTER 7

"Chase"ing the future.

Chase and I have known each other since infants. There hasn't been a day in my life that I haven't talked to him or seen him. Chase once told me that I was the sister he never wanted but was glad he had. When we were younger and our families would hang out Chase and his brother Ryan and I were together constantly. They often tortured me like brothers would torture a sister. I remember when I was thirteen and finally interested in boys. The Minella's had their annual 4th of July party and there were some cute boys there. I was finally able to fill out a bikini with a little confidence. For a small girl, I had a pretty good chest – a "C" cup. I wore my first real bikini that was more grown-up. The bikini was black and the bottom was high cut showing off my tanned legs. The top had spaghetti straps with small cups that really enhanced my ample cleavage. The center of the top had a gold embellishment. I felt like an actual teenager now. Mel was cracking up about my interest in boys and that I was crushing on one in particular. It was a guy named Robert Benson. He was the one I would become friendly with later when his parents were going through a divorce. He knew the Minella family through the hospital where both Sam Minella and my dad worked. I decided to strut past Robert and his friends who were hanging out pool side to catch his attention. Just as I got to where he was, he noticed for sure. I saw him smile at me and his dimples were adorable. He had on the latest Quiksilver board shorts and he was very well-toned and tanned.

"Hey Summer" said Robert and I started to turn to walk towards him so we could talk a little and get to know each other. That's when out of nowhere, Chase comes running up and pushes me into the pool. I didn't want to get my hair wet (you know for appearances purposes) and I had make-up on that had now run down my face and I looked like a clown when I resurfaced after being thrown into the pool. I could've killed Chase. Chase's brother Ryan laughed so hard he nearly peed in his pants. But, that was Chase. He was always torturing me. I was so embarrassed. I remember seeing Robert and his friends having a good laugh at my expense. I wanted to kill Chase that night. I yelled at Chase and told him he embarrassed me and he just said "good".

As much as Chase tortured me though, I knew he needed me and cared a lot about me too. During the first few years of college, there was more than one occasion that I had to help Chase get over a huge hangover before facing his parents. He also played a lot of head games with girls. He never seemed to find anyone that he truly wanted to be with. I wondered when he would break out of his lifestyle and grow up. Another part of me knew I would probably be the same way if I hadn't been forced to grow up so quickly. I wished who I was going to hook up with was on my top list of things to worry about. Mel and Chase pretty much lived at my house on weekends. Of course, it was really just the apartment part of the house though. I wouldn't really let anyone go in the main part of the house still except for Stella. Stella was like a night watchman. She didn't tell me but I knew she would wait up until I got home. I could see her peeking through her blinds and making sure I made it in safely. She didn't sleep at my house anymore ever since I graduated high school. Mel slept over often on the pull-out sofa couch and of course Chase slept in my bed with me. He spooned me like we were a couple. A couple of times in the morning I would wake up early and his hands were around me touching my chest if you know what I mean. He told me he was sleeping and didn't realize it. Hmmm...

Now that our final year of college was in session, we made the commitment to have as much fun as possible especially with each other. Working full-time was getting closer and closer and our lives would be over soon as we knew them. So, we figured we'd just have as much fun as possible. On Friday nights, it was mainly "game night" at my apartment. Chase, Mercer, Mel, Ronnie and some other friends from school would come over. We stocked the fridge with alcohol and I made some great finger foods and snacks. We often played Dilbert's Corporate Shuffle. It was a card game similar to a drinking game known as "Asshole". It's almost impossible to find and I only got it through ordering it off of E-bay and paying top dollar for it. But it is so worth it and is one of the best games we play. The premise was to get rid of your cards as fast as you can to climb the corporate ladder. Whoever was the "President" got to tell the others what to do. Robert Benson had come by to hang out too with some friends from medical school. He was the current Vice President in the game and the Vice President was a role that also had some power. Chase was President at the moment and I truly hoped I would take it away from him this round because I got some great cards as they were dealing and was hoping for a corporate take-over. I didn't like to look at my cards until they were completely dealt. I was superstitious about it. When my dad had played cards with me growing up, he did the same thing. I guess that's where I got it from. I had snuck a peak at one though and it was a wild card...one more wild card and I could become President.

It had become a tradition to have this game night during all of college. Somehow it always ended up being at my small apartment. I think they knew I would take the time to have food around and no one else would. The Minella and Wright families had game night too when my parents were alive. They played a card game called Canasta for hours upon hours every Friday night growing up while the kids all hung out and snuck onto the beach. It was nice to kind of do the same thing and I loved staying in and hanging out with my friends too. I was pretty competitive too and I wanted to become President since I spent most of the night as an intern tonight. As the cards were almost done being dealt, Robert asked me to get him a drink from the fridge since I was the intern.

"You better make it 2 beers" yelled Chase as the confident Mr. President.

I hoped so badly for my corporate take-over so I could order him around. I went to the refrigerator and grabbed two beers and walked back to the kitchen table to hand the boys their beers. Robert was pretty drunk already. I had never really seen him drunk before but he was pretty funny. I remembered how funny he was sober at the 4th of July fundraiser we went to when I was younger in Cape May. He was really drilling into Chase tonight with his jokes and Chase looked increasingly pissed off.

"Here is your drink Mr. President" I told
Chase and kissed him on the cheek
and rubbed his shoulders for a moment. "Here
is your drink Mr. Vice President"
and I handed Robert his beer. Robert asked
"where is my kiss and backrub"?
Chase looked red in the face. "The President
isn't allowing it" he chimed in…
"I have the authority remember"?!

The room got kind of quiet and uncomfortable. I sat down to look at my cards.

"Actually I have the authority" I said "Corporate Takeover!"
as I placed my 2 wild cards on the table.

Everyone was laughing and I had both Chase AND Robert get everyone a round of drinks as my first order as leader, much to their dismay!

Before you knew it, senior year was almost over. The football games, game nights, bar hopping and studying were keeping us busy all year. The holidays came and went. Chase had bought me a necklace that said "Summer" in diamonds. He told me it was to replace the one my parents had given me so many years ago that I lost. I really liked it and wore it all the time. Chase's mom Abbie was really always the one that gave me Christmas gifts each year. This was really the first time Chase had done something on his own for me and I couldn't help but notice how thoughtful it was. You can never go wrong with jewelry but I liked that he did it for sentimental reasons too. I cherished it. I couldn't get over how fast the year had gone by. It was mid-March now and the ocean was cold and there was still snow on the ground. It was Spring Break and everyone was going to Cabo, Cancun, Daytona Beach or the Bahamas. Chase, Mercer and I decided to do a "surfing spring break". Mel and Ronnie didn't have the money and chose to stay behind although I would've paid for Mel if she wanted to go but I think she liked having Ronnie all to herself sometimes which made me smile. The idea to do a "surfing spring break" came one night after game night was over and Mercer and Chase decided to crash at my place. We were just playing around on my iPad when we started googling the top surfing destinations in the world.

We thought about a lot of different places. Like Cabo San Lucas in Mexico was actually a destination that a lot of kids from our school and of course many other universities were going to. It was also a great surfing destination. There are other places with great surfing too like Portugal or San Juan, Puerto Rico. We had to pick somewhere good but not too crazy or too far. We had done the wild spring breaks and just wanted one a little different this year. Cabo kept coming back up because of its southern Baja location and all the beautiful California guys and girls that would be there. There was a place called Costa

Azul that was a little more low key. We could basically just stay at the beach instead and it was known for surfing and only a half hour away but at least a little away from the craziness.

We decided to do a surfing package at the Costa Azul Resort in Mexico. We had an ocean view room and all meals were included. We would surf in Punta Mita. This was their primary surfing destination and was an eight mile peninsula that we were taken to by boat to get the best waves. We could also surf at Costa Azul on their local break. The spring and summer there had the biggest waves of the season so we would knew we would have a ton of fun. We arrived in Costa Azul from a taxi from the airport after flying into Puerto Vallarta. It took about thirty minutes and we arrived in San Pancho, the small fishing village where the resort was located. The pool was over 20,000 gallons and lined the beach. They had a full wait staff that you could order drinks and relax. The beauty and pristine beaches were overwhelming. They had an open-air spa too and I couldn't help but think that I wanted to take advantage of that while I was here too. We mainly checked in, ate, drank and swam the entire first day. We wanted to just relax and take it all in. We ate dinner at Wahoo's restaurant, which was located at the resort while overlooking the Pacific Ocean. It was a casual atmosphere and we sat out on the deck overlooking the ocean. We stayed till the restaurant closed at 11:00 p.m. and then headed back to our room to get a good night's sleep before the early morning boat ride to Punta Mita.

After breakfast that morning, we met with the other surf excursion participants and headed out on the boat ride to Punta Mita with our boards. When we arrived, Mercer noted how the surf break was consistent and the waves were decent. I couldn't help but notice the water was crystal clear and tropical. Before we would go out, Chase, Mercer and I would huddle like football players. Mercer did a pep talk in our huddle.

"This is our time. This is our moment. The three of us are here together and we are going to look back some day and know that this was the time of our lives. Let's leave everything behind in Avon-by-the-Sea and just be here together. Just the three of us" said Mercer talking and acting deeper than I had ever seen him.

He was right. This week was our time. It was our chance to be together, probably one last time. Life was going to change. We had to get back to school, finish and graduate. Then, we would be working full-time and moving on with our lives. This was our last chance to be kids. This was our last chance to be in this kind of moment. We had no cares in the world. We just had a blast as three friends that had spent a lifetime together. Even though we knew there were nicer beaches all around us, this was THE place to surf. This is what we lived for. We went there each day all day. We sat in the water and watched the ocean sparkle in the sun. We rode waves and cheered each other on. We were never apart except to take a shower. We also went zip-lining, visited the open-air spa, horseback riding on the beach and visited all the local surf shops. On our last night, after dinner we went dancing at the resort where they had a DJ spinning what seemed like all hits from the 1980s. The song "Purple Rain" by Prince came on and Mercer grabbed me and Chase in a huddle again. We embraced in a huddle singing the song on top of our lungs and all three of us were crying and no one could break into our huddle. It was symbolic of the tight friendship we shared and would always share. I think we just knew deep down that this moment was ours and I loved Mercer for creating this moment that I would always remember. This was one of our last moments of our trip but nonetheless this moment was ours... as three friends who just simply love each other. This was our vacation of a lifetime. We shared our friendship and our love of surfing. Nothing could ever break us apart and this moment singing "Purple Rain" on the top of lungs as cheesy as it was, it was our time together. When we flew back on the plane and closed our eyes. I know all three of us reflected on the time we spent together. These were moments we would never forget and a time in our life we would never forget. I had never felt so lucky in my life to have my friends. I was really so very lucky. When we arrived in Newark Airport, Chase's parents had arranged for a car service to pick us up. We all sighed as we were driven back to reality at Avon-by-the-Sea.

Now it was the end of our senior year. We had only a week left till graduation and had to figure out what we were going to do with the rest of our lives. I thought I had it all figured out. I sat on the porch with a margarita in my hand and stared out at the ocean on my father's swing. I had been going to camps and working part-time at the aquarium since I was little and now I was working there again and running their camp program. They told me when I was ready, I could work full-time in any of their marine life exhibits and so could Mel and Ronnie. I knew that place like the back of my hand and was familiar with all of their protocols. I loved it there. It felt like a home to me more than a job and the animals were so much fun and I had grown to love and adore all of the kids in the camp programs and looked forward to seeing them every year. Plus, I had grown up going with Chase to summer camps there and it reminded me every time I pulled up of the times when my mom was dropping Chase and me off in the mornings for the camp program. It was nice to feel that memory in the air and it was such a fun time in my life spending camp days there.

I took a sip of the margarita. I loved the way the sea salt made the drink taste as I licked my lips. I had been feeling nostalgic since our trip for Spring Break. I started to think about all of my favorite times at the camp program growing up. My favorite time in camp was when Chase and I snuck late at night into the aquarium one summer. I think we were fourteen or fifteen and we were actually volunteers now helping the camp program since we knew it like the back of our hands. Ryan and Chase were sleeping over because their parents were away for the weekend and my parents were watching them. Everyone was fast asleep in the house. I remember when Chase and I snuck out through the apartment/bedroom that was empty at the time unlike today. We saw a bunch of kids riding the trolley to the clubs and snuck in the back so the driver wouldn't see two non-club age kids on there.

The trolley was great because it was free and it helped promote a safe community by not having people drink and drive. The aquarium was only around the corner from a popular night club in town so we hopped off and walked over once the driver made it to the club. Chase carried a large brown bag and wouldn't tell me what was in it. We knew the code for the back door and entered into the aquarium.

Chase made me close my eyes while he set up. I remember being so nervous that we would be caught and thrown into jail and end up in juvenile detention. When I opened my eyes, he had made a huge picnic by the penguin tank. We could have gotten arrested. It was awesome though. Chase thought of everything. He set up a blanket and had stolen little sandwiches that his mom had made for one of their nightly parties. He got my favorite dessert too from the local bakery – chocolate mousse. He also stole one of his parent's bottles of wine. Alcohol and I have never been a good combination. Maybe it's my size but one drink and I am a goner. In fact, Chase had to carry me home and sneak me into my bedroom because of that wine. It was a good thing I was small and light and he liked to carry me. We weren't used to drinking back then being only fourteen or fifteen and I have never really been able to drink much in general anyway. Even now, I would have a drink or two but stayed away from liquor in general except for my occasional margarita – my one weakness. I guess I never really wanted to lose control either. There was no one there to pick up the pieces for me like I did for Chase and his drunken nights. Chase told me he wanted me to get drunk that night. As I said, he was always torturing me. But despite the wanting to get me drunk, he had thought of everything else and there was something romantic about it. But, I tried to block that from my mind. I never wanted to ruin what Chase and I had. His friendship meant the world to me.

The aquarium held a lot of great memories and I couldn't imagine working any place else now that my college career was coming to an end. But, Ron Johnson, who ran the Cape May Beach and Wildlife Preservation Association, had offered me a job too. He had kept in touch with me through the years. I think he felt in some way responsible for my parent's death because it was his and my dad's event that we were on the way home from when they died. He wanted me to come to Cape May and run a fundraising group for him. It was an awesome opportunity but it would take me away from the daily routine of working with the marine animals and with the camp program which I was more passionate about. I enjoyed the fundraising events too but didn't want to let go of the hands-on work with the animals and kids. He said it was an open offer if I changed my mind and all I had to do was let him know. The truth is I couldn't imagine leaving Avon-by-the-Sea and especially Chase. Even though, it wasn't too far, I didn't want to leave my community just like my parents. There were so many memories here for me.

Images of surfing in Mexico filled my head. It was probably one of the best times I have ever had in my life. My mind just couldn't stop thinking and remembering probably because it was the end of an era. One other memory flashed in my mind as the alcohol from the margarita started to work its magic. This memory stands out for me because it's a surfing memory and surfing is one of my favorite pastimes. Another thing Chase and I did and never told my parents or his parents growing up was night surfing. When it was a clear night and the moon was bright, we would sneak our surf boards out and go night-surfing. It was pretty dangerous but it was something that we did and never told anyone, not Ryan or Mel. The only one who knew was Mercer because of course; he would be pissed if he couldn't come on occasion. We often did it during our parent's game nights because they were preoccupied for hours and didn't know what we were doing half of the time. Ryan was younger and usually asleep anyway so it was the perfect opportunity to not get caught. One time Chase and I got caught soaking wet but since Chase had the habit of throwing me into pools and the ocean, it was an easy excuse when he told them he tossed me into the ocean.

We didn't night surf often though. We only did it once in a while and it always seemed to be when something bad was happening in one of our lives. It was sort of like a dangerous escape from reality...living on the edge of disaster and no one knew about it. It was somewhere to go and think. The sounds of the ocean helped you meditate and it cleared your mind. It was truly exhilarating. We would sit out there on our boards floating in the water and talk for hours. We were out there a lot after my parents died too once my wrist had healed. When Chase was having trouble picking his major in school, we were out there. When I lost my favorite necklace that my parent's had given to me as a child that said my name – Summer – we were out there again. It was sort of our secret escape and meeting spot between the two of us and our sometimes crasher – Mercer. We never went out there alone though – it was our pact. We did it together just in case. The ocean is beautiful but also dangerous and we were smart enough to know that. None of us had ever broken that promise that I know of. We all wanted to avoid being pulled out to sea, getting attacked by sharks or getting injured somehow. The full moon helped shine the way. Somehow you found inner peace in those waters at night and the reward outweighed the risk. I liked how Chase would lock his arm in mine so that we would float together out there. I liked the way the moon shines on his body and his eyes. They were starting to sell neon stickers and these lights that glowed in the ocean to put on your board but Chase and I liked the idea of being in total darkness. You felt more at one with the ocean but we did think that in the future we should have a neon night surfing party. It must look really cool to watch someone surfing in the dark with a lit-up board.

 This senior year had been such a strange year. Chase had acted different towards me all year. It was like he was at a cross-road with something but couldn't share it with me. It hurt in a lot of ways because we had always shared everything with each other. He was with me constantly yet held back in some way with whatever it is that has been on his mind. I guess I was the same way too. I knew that life would change after college and a lot of us would start to really lead our own lives and it wouldn't be the same anymore. Maybe that scared Chase as it scared me too. Chase seemed to be cleaning up his act. He wasn't really hooking up with anyone anymore and he was drinking less. He was working hard at school and trying to figure out his career. He was finally turning things around and it was great to see. I was scared of the future in a lot of ways…but, I was excited to graduate and start my career and find out what the future had in store for me. I just needed to figure out my heart and why it hurt so badly. I was also at peace because Chase didn't have a girlfriend. I didn't want him with anyone even though I still had Brad stringing along all year. I needed to figure out why I felt that way once and for all. Sam had stopped by to see me earlier today to see how I was doing. The Minella's were such special people to me.

"Hi Summer!" said Sam joyfully as he came up on the porch.
"Hi Sam" I said and gave him a hug as he came up and sat next to me.
"Going out with the crew tonight to celebrate?" asked Sam.
"Yes, can't wait!" I told him cheerily "after dinner with Stella of course".
"Ahhh, yes. She is a good woman. How are things with
what's his name…Brad, isn't it?" he asked.
"Not very good. Coming to an end actually.
There was nothing really ever there to begin with" I told him truthfully.
"I think a lot of things are ending and new things beginning now.
Just got to follow your heart" said Sam "that's what I told Chase too".
"Chase isn't seeing anyone right now, right?" I asked Sam curiously.
"No. His heart seems to be taken from what I can see" Sam hinted.
"By who?" I asked wondering what he meant.
"You know Chase. He'll figure it out I am sure". "Have fun tonight and
we'll see you at graduation" said Sam smiling
and not wanting to say too much.

Sam left and I finished my margarita and went over to Stella's house to say hello to her and the dogs. I was cooking a special meal tonight and invited Stella over to join me before I went out later that evening with my friends. I took Bobby and brought him over to hang out with me and keep me company while I cooked dinner. This time I was making one of my mom's favorite recipes. It was a really simple recipe but a terrific dish and besides I liked to do nice things for Stella. She had done so much for me. I made a salad with greens, sliced red grapes, halved walnuts, sunflower seeds, raisins and tomatoes. I put raspberry vinaigrette dressing on it and sprinkled crumbled blue cheese on top. Then, I made a flank steak and sliced it thin and put the pieces on top of the salad ready to be served. Bobby got a few samples of the steak. Of course, we didn't tell Stella that part! It was an easy and delicious meal. Stella arrived and we enjoyed the meal and she talked about her son. She was such a proud mom.

> *"Brice is making that new movie. He is hopefully filming some of the scenes locally and I'll get to see him soon"* Stella glowed as she spoke of her son.
> *"You must be so proud of him Stella"* I replied happily.
> *"I am also so proud of you Summer. You are graduating. You have a job all lined up doing what you love. You have done an amazing job."* Stella said proudly.
> *"Thanks Stella. I couldn't have done it without you. I love you".*

She really was so proud of me for graduating soon and handling everything so well in my life. Her support means the world to me. I am glad she thought I had it altogether but inside I was empty. It was different than the emptiness I felt from the longing for my parents. It was an emptiness that I felt in my heart for love. I knew deep down that I already knew what I wanted in that department. I just hadn't been able to put the pieces of the puzzle together….yet.

> *"Brice and Tanya broke up"* Stella said smiling a devilish grin. *"He is dating a new girl now named Marcella and she also works behind the scenes".*
> *"I can't wait to meet her Stella. See everything works out in the end"* I told her happily.

Everything works out in the end....hmmm...I just hoped so much I was right. I could use a happy ending in my life. Sam's words about Chase's heart being "taken" worried and encouraged me. Maybe, just maybe, I had taken Chase's heart. It would be my perfect happy ending. But, what if it was someone else? I needed to know once and for all.

> "What about you Summer? Are you ever going to tell Chase you love him?" smiled Stella.
> I couldn't help but think she knew me so well as I responded "Oh Stella. I think I finally am actually. I plan on dumping Brad. I want to see if there is a future with Chase. I guess it's now or never".
> Stella hugged me and told me "Summer, he loves you and if he doesn't then he is a fool. You are the perfect catch and don't ever forget that."

I hoped she was right. Chase and I were both avoiders. We both kept a lot inside. We are very similar in that way. We both expected the other to do things versus taking responsibility. It's been like that our whole life. I thought of all our times together growing up and the special moments we shared. No one could ever take that away from me. I knew deep down that Chase was the one for me in my soul. After dinner, I went to go get ready for the evening and pulled out my journal. This time, I didn't look at my parent's picture. I just looked at the picture of Chase and I on the beach and smiled. He has always been my best friend. My everything. That Spring Break surfing with Mercer and Chase we had only lived in the moment. We didn't talk about Avon-by-the-Sea, school, our relationships or friends. We only embraced the moment we were in – surfing and with each other. I had spent my whole life living in the past or worrying about the future. I had to start embracing the moments and living in the right now. It was a revelation of sorts for me. I had to grasp my moment now before it was too late with Chase.

CHAPTER 8

Kissing for Amy

For the last four years while we were attending the University, our Saturday nights were pretty much spent at a bar on the beach called Martin's Bar and Restaurant. It was directly on the beach and there was the awesome trolley that you could take so no one had to worry about drinking and driving. Everyone from school and locally went there and it was a blast. I remember as kids Chase, Ryan and I would watch the trolley go by from the window of my house and couldn't wait for the day that we were allowed to go. Martin's was such a cool place. It was "the" place to be and the most popular around which according to Mercer meant more money for Brad if he chose to bartend here and how he found it funny that he didn't choose to do so. Martin's had bands play there often and sometimes held fundraising events for the community. Mainly it was a DJ and dance floor though on Saturday nights.

Brad was there a lot and we would hang out when he would show up late after working at the other bar. I still couldn't figure him out. Mercer hated him. He called him a BENNY. This was a common slang name for people who lived in North Jersey or NYC and only came down the shore in the summers. It was considered a derogatory term nevertheless and was often used by shore residents to describe tourists from the more northern parts of NJ, specifically New York City and its immediate suburbs (B- Bayonne, E- Elizabeth, N- Newark NY – New York hence "Benny"). Brad went to school down here though now and lived down here in campus housing but Mercer didn't care. Mercer had actually gotten into a fist fight once with Brad. He never did tell me why but they both seemed to hate each other. Mercer hated Brad and Chase hated Robert. I wondered why we just couldn't all get along. It seemed that any outsider wasn't welcome in our inner circle. Except for Ronnie…he was welcomed with open arms thankfully for Mel.

It was a Saturday night at the end of June and we were completely done with finals at school and graduating next week so everyone was in a party mood. Stella had left after having dinner with me and I had just got done cleaning up the dishes and table. Everyone from school was going to Martin's later that night to celebrate before graduation. I decided to drive because I thought about going out to a diner after our night was over with Mercer and Chase after dropping Ronnie and Mel off. I didn't really drink anyway so I didn't have to worry about that. Mel had just arrived at my apartment. She had come over early to get ready and we were in my bathroom doing our hair and make-up. I had bought this new Roxy white sundress that I wanted to wear too and had just put it on.

"We are finally done with school and can get on with our lives. Woo hoo!" cheered Mel. "And you are going out in style. You look amazing Summer" she said and I gave her a hug.

I envied Mel. She had it all figured out, she knew she would work at the aquarium with Ronnie and they would be together and eventually get married. I had the education part done, a roof over my head, lots of money in the bank and the job situation handled but the "love" part….not so much. Tonight I was going to end it with Brad, if there was anything to even end. I barely saw him anyway. I wanted to leave that behind and look forward to the future and find my prince charming eventually too. I hated to do it though because I hated hurting people but I knew in the long run, I was putting off the inevitable.

"I am so glad you are leaving Brad behind with your days at Monmouth University" said Mel relieved.
"I know, I know, it's about time" I responded nervously.

I smoothed mango mandarin lotion on my legs and arms. It was my favorite and Chase's favorite too. Chase once told me he loved the way I smelled in this lotion. I used their shampoo and conditioner too in this fragrance. It was just such a refreshing scent.

"Not all of us have it all figured out Mel. You don't realize how lucky you are to have Ronnie".
Mel laughed. "I realize it Summer. I just want the same for you. You deserve better than him. There is just something slimy and sneaky that I get from Brad.
It's just a vibe" Mel said sounding concerned.
"The same vibe as Mercer and I guess myself too" I responded.
"Soon it will be a thing of the past".

Mel and I looked at ourselves in the mirror. We knew we would look back at these days and all the fun we had....our Friday night game nights and our Saturdays at Martin's...Mel sleeping over all the time. I didn't want it to end. Mel could tell I was looking nostalgic as we looked at ourselves in the mirror and she gave me a hug. Thank God for Mel. She was truly a gem of a friend.

Mel and I jumped into my Jeep and picked up Mercer, Chase, and Ronnie and we all headed over to Martin's. Chase and Mercer of course went right to the bar when we arrived and ordered beers. Mel and Ronnie headed over to the lounge area and sat on a sofa getting all snuggly and cutesy. I sat next to them and just watched them for a moment. Those two were so in love. Since Ronnie worked with both

Mel and me too, and we went to school together in the same major, I had gotten to know him better. He was so good to Mel and I was happy she found someone wonderful. My thoughts shifted to Brad. Brad was coming later after doing an earlier shift at the bar where he worked. He switched his schedule around to party with all of us since it was one of the last times we would be doing this altogether before our real lives began and school days were over. I cared and didn't care that he was coming. I don't know why. Maybe I was afraid to find the love like my parents had only to have it end so suddenly and I never really gave him a chance. It gave me some comfort that my parents had died together. I don't think either one could've survived without the other. I looked around the bar and couldn't help but think this was all getting too old. And I was getting really tired of watching Chase hook up with various girls every weekend. I guess you could say I was jealous. I knew I kind of was but I didn't want to believe it. Like now, up by Mercer and Chase at the bar, there was a girl by Chase's side already. It was Amy. How could I grasp my moment and tell Chase the truth if she was always in my way.

Yes, surprise, surprise, Amy was here too not that she shouldn't be – she was graduating too. She was up at the bar hanging out with Chase. I swear she was like a shark after her prey. Chase kept looking over at me as if he wanted me to rescue him. I couldn't help but notice how good he looked tonight. He had on a button-up Billabong white shirt with khaki short and slide-on Vans sneakers. He was looking over at me as if he wanted to talk to me about something. It was just a feeling I got in my gut. I smiled at him but he kept that serious look on his face. Sam's words were still ringing in my ears. Did Chase's heart belong to Amy? I just couldn't imagine it.

Chase knew it was now or never. School was done. He was done playing scared with Summer. He needed to make his move. "I just have to find the right time to do it" thought Chase as he half-listened to Amy and her friend. Mercer could sense the tenseness in the air coming from Chase too. He knew why. Chase didn't have to tell him although Chase finally had told him the truth when they were in Mexico. It was obvious anyway. Mercer laughed inside a little at it all. He knew what he had to do.

I told Mel and Ronnie I would be right back and walked towards the bar where they were to order my one drink that I was going to allow myself to have for the night since I was driving and had already had a drink before dinner. I really went up by them not to hang out but to see what was going on with Chase. I ordered my drink and while I waited for it I couldn't help but think that Chase should just end it once and for all with Amy. But, who am I to talk, I was stringing Brad along. At least tonight was the night though that Brad and I would finally come to end. Mel was proud of me for finally putting that behind me. I couldn't wait to get it over with but was dreading it too. I hated conflict. Chase did too which is probably why he couldn't hurt Amy's feelings…..unless there was more to his feelings for her…

Amy's friend pulled her to go to the ladies' room once I arrived by Chase and Mercer. She was always avoiding me. The bartender handed me my one drink….a margarita on the rocks with salt (again) and I took a sip. I love margaritas. That's when Mercer said he had a brilliant idea.

"You guys should start dancing and acting like you are together if you know what I mean"
said Mercer looking at me and Chase.
"It will finally give Amy the hint and she'll leave Chase alone"
"Oh my God, that's perfect!" screamed Chase with a wink towards Mercer.
"I need to get that girl off my back. I made out with her like twice in the past five years and she still won't leave me alone".

I downed my margarita. I don't know if it was my nerves or what really came over me. My head started to spin a little since I wasn't used to drinking and now technically had two drinks in my system. I saw Amy coming from the bathroom with her friend. Chase and Mercer grabbed my arm and dragged me out onto the dance floor to follow through on Mercer's plan. I kept reminding myself to live in the moment and stop thinking. Little did I know what was coming next...

The music was pounding a lot of club music and top-40 hits. We were dancing like crazy fools and the buzz from the margarita helped. Chase and I were dancing with each other. Chase was actually a pretty good dancer. Mercer had found some cute girl who looked like another surfer type that he was grinding up against. It must have been love at first sight because the next thing I know he is gone and so is that surfer chick. Ronnie and Mel watched from the couch where they just hung out and relaxed probably laughing at us.

The music changed to a slightly slower song. Chase gives me a little spin and then grabs me and pulls me in close. I couldn't help but think that I always felt so safe and comfortable in his arms. As we slow danced, he rubbed my back and seemed to lean in and smell my hair. Must be the mango mandarin, I thought to myself. He whispered to me that Amy was watching.

> *"I would grind with you but I am so short that you will be grinding into my stomach" I told him as we both laughed. "I love that you are small" Chase replied.*
> *"Maybe you should grab my butt instead"*
> *I told him with a smile whispering into his ear.*

But, he did it without hesitation. He moved his hands massaging me down my back and reached my butt and squeezed it while he hugged me closer and I thought I heard him moan a little when he did it. I tried not to laugh and give our prank away so I managed to just smile and hold it in.

> *I whispered to him "I'll do whatever takes to finally get her off your back".*
> *"Anything?" said Chase slyly.*

I ran my fingers through his hair. Then, I gave him small kisses along his neck and cheek. The alcohol gave me a little more confidence than I would normally have not that I seemed to need it. He turned towards me and looked at me directly in the eyes. His eyes were a hazel green and I loved the color. His sandy blonde hair was a little longer than usual and I liked it that way. He looked so serious though. I don't even think I recognized this look in him. Maybe he wanted to tell me he was in love with Amy. She had captured his heart. My heart hurt at the thought of it.

"Are you o.k., Chase?" I asked trying to figure out this look I saw in him.
"In this moment, I'm perfect" answered Chase.

Chase leaned his head towards me and our foreheads touched and I shut my eyes. I played with the back of his hair in my hands while he moved his hands down my back and to my waist. It was in that moment that I went back to a prior moment. The moment in the car driving with my parents from Cape May right before the accident had happened had flashed into my mind. I had closed my eyes that night in the car on our way back from Cape May and thought of Chase. I wanted to meet up with him and steal him away to enjoy the dessert I stole from the party. I remember thinking that I wanted to be with just him that night and was glad Mel had left in a way and that only Mercer was still there. I was starting to realize that more and more at the time and wanted to talk to him about it that night when I got there. I had wanted to see if he had any of those thoughts too. The cruise vacation we went on had so many wonderful moments but a lot of confusing ones too. I had wanted to talk to him about it to see what he thought. I never got my chance because my life was thrown in a different, unexpected way because of a rainy night and a careless driver.

It was now within this moment that I realized something I had always known...I loved Chase as more than a friend, and not in the brotherly kind of way either. I felt good in his arms because I was in love with him. It wasn't a brotherly kind of comfort in his arms; it was a romantic kind of comfort. I was just so afraid of him. The empty feeling I had at dinner with Stella was the spot that I wanted Chase to fill. I always wondered if he may be so close to me in all he does because he feels sorry for me, for my loss and the way my life has turned out. I could just end up being his "girl of the week" and tossed aside too. All I knew is I wanted him so badly in this moment but I was so scared of him as we danced still moving our hands around each other's bodies. My eyes were full of tears that I fought back. I hugged him and wiped one of my tears away so that he wouldn't notice and he lifted me in the air a little and pushed me into him. Chase then pulled me to face him again and gave me a small brief kiss as the song ended. I closed my eyes.

"Chase?" I said as I opened my eyes and looked at him.
Chase looked at me holding my hands in his and said "Summer?".

Chase and I stared at each other in silence for a brief moment both trying to find the words as the song ended and a new one was beginning. Mercer and his new chick came up to us. "Hi, I'm Marnie. You guys are so cute together" she said. Marnie was adorable. She was small like me and had long brown hair almost down to her waist with blonde highlights in it. Chase and I still sort of just stared at each other and didn't even acknowledge her.

Mercer jumped in and put his hand on Chase's shoulder
pulling Chase and I apart and said "Dude,
this totally worked. Amy is downstairs on the outer
level with her friends and looks upset.
I think you finally gave her the hint once and for all".
Mel came up and grabbed me and pulled me
down the stairs and outside asking
"What the heck happened there?!"

I filled her in on the plan to piss Amy off.

*"It was Mercer's idea that Chase and I act like we are
together so that Amy will leave Chase alone once and for all"
I told Mel trying to convince myself that's all it was.
"I saw more than that going on there Summer" said Mel excitedly.*

Before I could talk to her though, Chase was back.

*"Summer, can I talk to you for a moment"
Chase said with a serious tone as he
grabbed my hand and pulled me away from Mel who smiled at me.
"Listen, Amy still seems interested and I really need
to seal the deal Summer" Chase rambled.*

I didn't even see Amy anywhere in sight. How could she seem interested in him at this moment. She wasn't even around.

*"What do you mean by sealing the deal?" I inquired.
Chase responded very simply - "with a kiss".
"Are you in love with Amy?" I asked scared.
"Hell no" responded Chase "not even close Summer".*

I couldn't really even speak. I wanted to kiss him really badly but I also didn't want to. I was afraid I would feel something so incredible and it would be so painful when he didn't feel the same way. After all, he had once told me that I was the "sister" he never wanted but was glad he had. Is that how he saw me…as a sister? He has had so many chances to try something with me and he never did. I felt like I was losing my mind. It would feel almost as terrible as losing my parents if I were to lose Chase in my life. Chase was everything to me just as my parents were my whole life. It was the reason why I had pulled a picture of him and me together along with my parent's wedding picture and put it in my journal. Before I could ask him anything else, he pulled me around a corner and pushed me up against the wall.

All I could ask is "how is Amy going to see us back here"?
Chase said "she has x-ray eyes, trust me Summer".

I didn't have any time to respond...Chase leaned right in and kissed me with no hesitation whatsoever. Soft small kisses at first and it was none short of amazing when I felt his lips brush mine. I felt weak and the whole room disappeared as if we were the only two people here. My stomach felt like butterflies and those small kisses felt better than sex. The chemistry blew me away. I have never had a kiss like this in my life. I don't really know what got into us but it progressed quickly from there. Passion took over and the next thing I know we were making out pretty intensely. It was like we had held it in for so long and it was finally happening or so I wanted to believe. He tasted perfect and I have never kissed anyone with this intensity in my life. Our tongues viciously moved in our mouths. I ran my fingers through his hair and down his back and squeezed him closer. His hands were all over me too in all the most inappropriate places. It was more than a kiss. I felt like he wanted me as badly as I wanted him. Our lips parted and he moved to my neck and kissed me there. I gasped for air almost moaning and could barely breathe. He grabbed my breasts and kissed my cleavage and then went back to my lips as our tongues intertwined. We stopped for a brief moment, almost as if we were out of breath and we looked at each other and then Chase pulled me closer and hugged me smelling my hair again.

"God Summer. You are so incredible" said Chase winded.
"Kissing you is amazing Chase" I said breathless and shocked.

I could hear Mel and Mercer yelling that Brad was there and coming over but it sounded a million miles away. Chase leaned in and kissed me again and grabbed my butt and pushed me into him and I could feel him pulsating for me and I just moaned a little because I wanted him so badly.

"Brad's coming dude" said Mercer frantically.
"Summer, he is going to see you guys!" yelled Mel.

Chase abruptly backed away from me looking at me dead on into my eyes out of breath.

"Chase?" I said frantically wanting to tell him I loved
him but that's all I was able to say being
out of breath and in shock of the passion we just shared together.
"Summer, I..." was all Chase got out.

Brad came around the corner in that moment.

"There you are" said Brad as he kissed me on
the cheek and put his arm around me.
"Hi" was all I was able to manage.

Chase grabbed Mercer and took off. I told Brad I wasn't feeling well all of a sudden and grabbed Mel and ran to the bathroom. Brad followed and was waiting outside the door, appearing worried. In the bathroom, I confessed to Mel how I felt although I could tell it wasn't really a surprise to her. She had witnessed the kiss and the look on our faces. I told her that my whole life I was in love with Chase but now with that kiss knew it for sure.

"That was WAY more than a kiss Summer" Mel said elatedly.

She was right....it was. I couldn't be just a friend to him any longer and that scared me. She was thrilled and scared for me at the same time. She knew I had been through so much pain in my short life. I told her that the reason I pushed men away was because in my heart I was hoping that Chase would someday fall in love with me.

"A part of me felt like I have been with Chase my whole life anyway

> *and I don't need anyone else nor do I really want*
> *anyone else. I never have" I shared with Mel.*
> *Mel hugged me. "Summer, he looked like he was in love with you too.*
> *You should've seen him kissing you" said Mel. "I hope you are right Mel."*

But Chase is known for his ways with women. Was I just another woman? I thought back to when I had woken up in the hospital the night my parents died.

> *"The night of the accident when I woke up in the*
> *hospital, I was calling out for Chase.*
> *The nurse had told me" I confessed to Mel.*

I started to ramble as all of these thoughts entered my head...

> *"And, remember when we were younger too, how he pushed me in the*
> *pool in front of Robert Benson and how he texted me*
> *calling Robert an a**hole? And showing up in*
> *Cancun? Maybe he was jealous??*
> *And remember the pink roses at the beach with the kids during camp?"*
> *Mel agreed laughing. "Slow down!*
> *It seems to make sense though. I have always thought it*
> *too. Chase is so bad at expressing his feelings.*
> *Maybe those were his ways of showing you" shared Mel.*

Maybe it was just all making sense now and the pieces were coming together. I have always loved him and needed him. Now, I wanted him so badly. But maybe, just maybe, he felt the same way.

> *"Or, maybe I am reading too much into it and*
> *it's all in my mind" I told Mel.*
> *"The truth is you won't know unless you confront*
> *Chase and ask him" said Mel.*
> *"He seemed like he wanted to talk but you got interrupted" she finished.*

By now Mercer had come looking for me. Chase had sent him. Chase wanted to talk to me but Brad was outside the door so he sent Mercer to get me.

"Where's Summer?" asked Mercer.
"She is in the bathroom" said Brad with rudeness in his voice.

Brad told me Mercer was a waste of life which I hated Brad for saying. Just because Mercer would rather live his life on a surfboard didn't mean anything except he has a passion for it. I always admired Mercer for doing what he enjoyed most in life and sticking to it. Mercer stood across the way waiting for me too. Mercer thought "lucky me, forced to hang out with Brad". Brad's friend John came up.

"Dude what's up?" said John.
"Waiting for the bitch that's going to pay my bills someday to come out of the bathroom" said Brad.

It was all Mercer could take. He had fought Brad before over Summer. Chase didn't want Brad and Summer together and had Mercer learn as much as he could about Brad since he saw him often in classes at school and Chase was away in Europe at the time and couldn't do anything to stop it. Mercer knew Chase didn't want anyone with Summer in tact. He was always making sure no one could have what he shared with Summer. Mercer wished Chase would tell Summer once and for all how he has always felt about her. This was finally Chase's opportunity and he finally had the courage to do it. Mercer thought his idea of pissing off Amy was really to just force Summer and Chase to finally confront their feelings. It was so obvious their hearts were in it for more than friendship. Brad was the obstacle. Mercer had learned earlier in the year that Brad was cheating on Summer and punched him in the face. Mercer and Chase had gone to the bar that Brad bartends at and saw him with another girl. Mercer and Chase didn't have the heart to tell Summer. She had lost so much already and they figured they could scare Brad away or she would realize it on her own eventually. This time, Mercer was done though and he lunged at Brad and knocked him on the ground.

> "You are such a prick. Is that what you are
> after, her money?" Mercer asked.
> "What's it to you?" snarled Brad.

The two struggled with each other and several bouncers came up and separated them. Mel and I heard a commotion outside the bathroom and heard some girls yelling "fight"! We quickly ran for the bathroom door and saw Mercer on top of Brad.

> "Oh my God" yelled Mel.

I didn't know why they were fighting and Mercer was thrown out by a bouncer before I could talk to him. All I could hear was one thing that Mercer yelled.

> "Brad is not the guy for you Summer" yelled Mercer.
> "What the hell is going on here? Why are you
> and Mercer fighting?" I questioned
> Brad as I helped him to his feet.
> The bouncer grabbed Brad's arm – "you need
> to leave" the bouncer chimed in.
> "I was jumped by him" screamed Brad. "I don't care" said the bouncer.
> "It's not worth it Brad, I'll walk you out to leave" I told him.
> "Aren't you going to come with me?" Brad
> asked. "No" was all I could get out.

I needed to talk to him now and not waste any more time. He wasn't the one for me and never would be. I knew now more than ever and that made it so much easier to tell him. There had to be a reason Mercer didn't like him too and I was sure Mercer was standing up for me when he fought Brad tonight and in the past. Even without the fight, I had set my mind on ending things tonight and it was now or never. The bouncer told Brad he had to leave and I didn't want to delay it any further so I walked with him towards the front door...

Chase saw Summer pass by walking with Brad. They had their arms hooked and seemed to be heading out with each other. It was more than Chase could handle.

"Where the hell is Mercer?" Chase said impatiently to Marnie who was next to him waiting for Mercer too. "I don't know. Something must have happened. I saw a commotion up there and he is taking really long" responded Marnie who was looking around anxiously for Mercer.

Chase wanted to tell Summer he loved her and always has but he thought that she was into Brad more than him by seeing her leave with him and he just couldn't take it. Chase downed two shots in a row as Amy walked up to him.

"What's going on, Chase? Are you with Summer? I saw you guys dancing on the dance floor" Amy questioned. "No, she is with Brad", Chase said frustrated ordering another shot. "You don't know that for sure" said Marnie. "I am going to find Mercer" said Marnie as she walked off. Amy smiled coyly and said "I am glad Summer is with Brad. I think you know I have always had a thing for you. We are graduating now and well since you aren't with Summer after all, well, you won't mind if I do this then...".

Amy leaned in eagerly and kissed Chase on the lips.....

I stood in the front doorway with Brad and told him that it was over.

*"I can't do this anymore Brad. The reason I
never got exclusive with you is because
in my heart I knew we weren't a perfect fit. I'm
sorry to do this to you in a doorway.
This isn't how I planned it and I care about
you but I don't see a future together.
I didn't think it would be fair to keep you hanging on
any longer and I am so sorry" I told Brad.
"You are over-reacting Summer. Mercer just doesn't
like me. It has nothing to do with you".
The bouncer was pulling me back in and I yelled
back "I'll talk to you more later. I just can't
explain right now" I responded. "What do you
mean this isn't how you "planned" it?
You had planned this discussion? If you care
about me at all, you'll come outside
and talk to me now. I love you Summer".*

It was true I had planned it but I wasn't going out there. I knew it was pointless and although harsh, I had to get to Chase. I only told Brad right there and then because I wanted to tell him before anything further happened with Chase. I needed to start over with a clean slate. I ignored Brad and walked back inside with the bouncer. I could see Brad standing outside waiting and wondering if I would return to talk to him. I wouldn't be.

I ran inside to find Chase. I couldn't wait to find him. While it was scary and I didn't know how he would react, I couldn't keep it in. I smiled as I ran over to the stairwell to look for him despite all that had happened with the fight and breaking up with Brad. I couldn't contain it. It was the first time since before my parents had died that I had smiled and really meant it. Was it that I was finally finding happiness in my life again? It felt so good. I saw Mel on the way and told her I dumped Brad. She hugged me…

> "I am so proud of you Summer. Now let's go find him!"
> Mel said enthusiastically referring to Chase.

We ran over to the top of the stairs to scan the room for Chase.

> "I hope he hasn't left to find Mercer" said Mel.

I looked over by the bar where we had been hanging out earlier. I wished I hadn't looked at that bar because I just couldn't believe my eyes. Mel saw it at the same time because I could see the look on her face out of the corner of my eye. Amy and Chase were kissing.

> "What the hell" I whimpered to Mel softly as Ronnie
> walked up to see what was going on.

I didn't have any energy anymore. It was like air let out of a balloon and the balloon gets smaller and smaller. That's how I felt – small and deflated. The room started to spin and I felt dizzy. Mel grabbed me and I ran back into the bathroom with her leaving Ronnie trying to figure out what was happening.

> "I really am just another girl to him. I can't believe it."

I just fell into Mel's arms. I couldn't help but feel sorry for myself. Why did others have it all and I have nothing or no one?

> "I have to get out of here" I said pushing Mel away.
> "I am not taking any chances of having to see
> him and Amy again" I said as I
> climbed out the bathroom window and landed
> on the sand with Mel yelling at me
> not to jump and that I would hurt myself. I did it anyway.
> "Are you going to be o.k.? Let me get Ronnie
> and we'll meet you outside" yelled Mel.

"No Mel! I want to be alone. I am fine." I cried.

Mel told me to wait but I didn't listen. I ran across the sand and up the stairs to the boardwalk and out to the street. I hoped to God that Brad was nowhere in sight and I made it to my car and took off.

The others could take the trolley home. I needed to 'escape'. How could I be such a fool to think that I had a chance with Chase. He would never settle down. He was a player – plain and simple – and he probably just felt sorry for me because my parents were dead and that he owed me something because our families grew up together. That's why he was always so involved in my life. I was such a fool. He probably only kissed me because he liked the attention Amy gave him and he used me to push her over the edge. He used me. He never did say it was for any other reason. How could I have let him into my heart in the romantic way. My heart pained so badly as I drove home. The fifteen minute ride felt like it was taking forever. Tears were streaming down my face and I sobbed uncontrollably. I hadn't cried this hard in a long time. It was just so much pain again. I just love him so much more than I ever thought I could. It hurt in the way it hurt when I lost my parents. A hurt that I knew could never be fixed. I would never have Chase…just as I will never have my parents back.

CHAPTER 9

An Unexpected Call

I pulled my Jeep into the driveway at my house after leaving the club. My cheeks were still wet from my tears and my eyes hurt. Crying hard always brought me back to the tears I had shed and still shed for my parents. You cry so hard that your eyes hurt, your face is raw and you almost get numb when you finally stop. It was still early on Saturday night. It's hard to believe all that had happened in less than two hours of being there. What was supposed to be a night to remember…our fun night out after finals, making a clean break from Brad, the last hurrah before our future…turned out to be a night I wanted to forget. I wiped my tears away and got out of my car. I could see Stella watching from her window with Bobby on her lap as I climbed the stairs to my apartment. I didn't care and didn't even say hello or wave and just pretended I couldn't see her. Nothing seemed to matter to me anymore. I had lost Chase. I had lost my parents. Maybe I should leave this town once and for all. I entered my apartment and saw my wet suit hanging there. Should I? I pulled on my wet suit. I didn't even bother to change my dress and just pulled up the zipper to my wet suit right over the dress. I was about to break our golden rule and go night surfing……..alone. I needed to think. I couldn't take it anymore. Why had my life turned out this way? What did I do that my parents were taken from me and that Chase didn't love me? What was wrong with me? Is this the life that was planned for me? Everyone would look at me and think I had it all…money in the bank, a house on the beach, the best clothes and cars. If only they really knew the hell I lived in.

Stella would've stopped me but she had no idea what I was doing. She thought I was home and safe. We had enjoyed a lovely dinner and she knew I was in a good mood. She had nothing to suspect. I took a deep breath and told myself I was doing the right thing. Nothing was going to happen to me and if it did, maybe it was for the best. Maybe my suffering would end. I had walked down through the inside of the house and went through the front door so Stella wouldn't see me leave and then snuck and grabbed the board. My phone rang as I made it out the driveway and was about to cross the street to the beach. I was afraid to look at it. I didn't feel like dealing with Brad begging me to come back or Mel filling me in on what Chase was doing with Amy now. I hoped it wasn't Stella wondering where I was going. I just thought that I should've just left my phone inside the house. I glanced at my phone and it was an unexpected person – it was Robert Benson.

I decided to answer which I am not sure why given the mood I was in. I hadn't talked to Robert in a while and wanted to have someone to talk to. Plus, Chase hated him so much and it gave me pleasure to know I was talking to him behind Chase's back at this very moment. I knew Robert was probably at his mom's house this weekend. She had bought a home in Avon-by-the-Sea about two blocks in from the beach and was living not too far from me.

"Hey Robert" I answered despondently.
"Hey Summer! I am staying this weekend at my mom's house" Robert told me.
"I went over to Martin's to meet up with you guys but I couldn't find you anywhere".
"I left Robert" I explained unenthusiastically. "I just grabbed my board and was heading up to the beach".

I was so distraught and Robert could hear it in my voice. I needed someone to talk to and Robert had become a good friend. Maybe he should be my new night surfing partner. I didn't have Chase anymore.

*"You can meet up with me if you are willing to throw
on a wetsuit and grab a board" I asked him.
"No, Summer. Mercer once told me about your night
surfing escapades" said Robert sounding
concerned. It's too dangerous. I'm a horrible surfer in daylight and
I don't want you going out there alone".
"I need to think Robert" I told him sounding dismal.
"You sound frantic Summer. What's wrong?" he
asked sounding more and more concerned.*

I didn't know what to say to him. He didn't know how I felt about Chase. I didn't want him to necessarily know. I didn't know how to respond.

*"It's Chase. He put me in an awkward spot tonight.
Also, I am at a crossroads with the job front...
I am thinking about leaving and going to Cape
May for the job in fundraising."*

I wasn't sure where that even came from but I guess I just wanted to run away once and for all. Robert told me to stay where I was.

"If you need to think, let's do it together. We have always talked each other through our problems. Don't make this problem any different" he told me.

I waited on my front porch while he drove to my house from the club. He pulled up in his Silver Volvo SUV. Silver, of course, I thought to myself…just like my dad would've wanted. He was the perfect guy. I threw my surfboard on the ground near my car and got into his car. I looked terrible. My make-up was smeared, my new white Roxy dress was dirty and a mess from jumping out of the window of the bathroom at Martin's and was now at least hidden under a wet suit of all things and most of all, I was just sad and not at all fun to be around.

"Hey Summer" said Robert and he gave me a hug as I got in the car.
"I know, I look like the girl of your dreams right now" I said sarcastically knowing I looked a mess. Robert just smiled and said "just maybe you are. Hard to resist a girl in a wet suit".

Robert could find humor in anything, I thought. Robert took me to the bay side to a playground. We got out of the car and he put me in a headlock making fun of me and saying "my poor Summer is upset". It should've been funny. I knew he was trying to cheer me up but it just wasn't working. We went over onto the playground and we sat on the swings in silence.

"So? Are you going to fill me in?" Robert finally asked.

I stared at my feet and then looked up at the stars and then finally, I became overcome with emotion and just had to share it with him. He was such a good listener and always has been. He was perfect to talk to too because he wasn't involved in the evening's events and I decided to share the truth with him. Tears rolled down my face as I broke down and told him everything that had transpired earlier in the night. The plan to piss off Amy, dancing with Chase, the kiss Chase and I shared, breaking up with Brad and just feeling an overall sadness tonight. He didn't say a word the entire time. Robert just looked at me and smiled and grabbed my hand when I finally stopped talking.

"I can't believe you are smiling right now!" I
told him wiping my tears away.
"I've always had a little crush on you Summer.
From when we were kids at the

*Minella family parties or through the fundraising events we attended
with our families, but I was told from a young
age you were off-limits....by Chase".*
"What?" I asked. "What do you mean?"
*"You know Chase has had a thing for you his entire life.
He told me on multiple occasions that I could
have any girl in the world but you.
I kept the promise although I never wanted to.
Remember, he even said I was away
prom weekend? I was in town the whole time.
He just didn't want you to ask me.
I called you tonight because I wanted to ask you out once and for all.
You are done with school and I have a few years left of medical school.
You and Chase never got together so I figured that here was my shot and
I was tired of obeying him for no real good reason.
I don't owe anything to Chase and I have always
wanted to get to know you better.
Not that we don't know each other but you know what I mean".*

I couldn't believe my ears. I really liked Robert but I wasn't sure if I could ever love anyone like I loved Chase and why exactly had Chase made me off limits from a guy like Robert only to turn around and kiss Amy if he loved me so much. I was too exhausted to think.

*"Maybe Chase is playing the ultimate head game with me.
He loves to play head games with girls and maybe he has just saved the
ultimate grand finale of his single days for me"* I said aloud to Robert.
*"He knows you have it all, the looks, the future, the smarts, the money and
Chase knew I could really end up liking you if
we got to know each other more".*

I thought about my parents. They would have loved Robert. He was smart and handsome. He was caring, thoughtful and funny. Maybe I should do what makes sense. They would've been disappointed in

Chase's behavior…hooking up with girls, torturing me. Chase's heart didn't seem to be with "me" after all or he never would've kissed Amy after kissing me. Robert grabbed my hand and pulled me up from the swing.

"Can I kiss you Summer?" he asked hopeful pulling me closer to him.

I wasn't sure if I should or even if I wanted to but maybe I should…it would be nice to have someone to take care of me for once and not have me take care of them like I did for Chase my whole life. Plus, a guy like Robert made sense. And, he was such a great person.

"I just want to see if there is chemistry or a spark there and then we can move forward or put it behind us" pleaded Robert. All I could think of was Chase kissing Amy so I said "let's try it and see what happens".

Robert pulled me close to him and then he leaned towards me and brushed my hair out of my face. Robert was so handsome and sweet. He was smart and funny. He was the perfect guy who deserved the perfect girl. He pulled me close and we looked into each other's eyes. Robert kissed me tenderly under the light of the moon and the stars. It should have been a magical moment. He kissed me so softly and romantically. He was a good kisser too but after a moment had passed I just couldn't do it. Sadly, I felt like I was betraying Chase and even worse myself. I pulled away. I wasn't Robert's perfect girl and that wasn't fair to him.

"I'm sorry Robert. My heart is somewhere else". "I like you so much as a friend but I just can't do this right now" I said as the tears rolled down my cheeks as I looked down and stared at my feet. "I understand" said Robert. "It's Chase isn't it?" he asked.

I just nodded my head with a yes. And, yes, it was Chase. I couldn't seem to escape him. Robert said he understood. He hugged me and we walked over to his car and he drove me home. The two minute drive was so awkward and I felt so sad that I couldn't be the one for Robert. He smiled and joked in the car like his usual self. He was so resilient. I thanked him for his friendship and for listening to me. We were still on good terms. He was such a class act. I hoped I wasn't disappointing my parents. Robert and I had always just been friends anyway and the magic just wasn't there in our kiss. Maybe he felt that too. We pulled up in front of the house and he gave me a hug and I got out of the car.

"Go inside and change and relax. Tomorrow things will look up. Everyone has a bad night" Robert yelled from his window.
"I know you were vulnerable tonight. My timing is horrible.
I'm sorry Summer" Robert said thoughtfully.
"It's not your fault Robert. You are such an awesome guy. It's me. I am a mess right now.
I am the one who is sorry" I told him.

I watched Robert pull away and stood there for a few minutes. I knew I wasn't making a mistake but Robert was a catch. And a good catch indeed. Any girl would be so lucky to have him. He was the total package so why couldn't I have those feelings for him. It would make things so much easier.

I snuck into the house through the front door so that Stella wouldn't see me. I thought about the brief kiss Robert & I shared. Maybe if we had dated from a young age, we wouldn't have known the difference and been together. Robert was such a great guy. I knew now more than ever that the kiss I shared with Chase though was something out of a fairy tale. I couldn't go backwards from there; not that being with a man like Robert would be going backwards. He just deserved someone who felt about him the way I felt about Chase. There would never be a kiss that felt like that again in my life. It really was amazing. It felt like we were just meant to be together. Kind of like the way my parents always described their love for each other. They just "knew". If I was not going to have Chase in that way, I needed to accept it and move forward. I was good at moving forward. When you have no choice, you would be amazed what you can do. I would focus my energies into something else like I have always done. I was good at ignoring the hurt and pain I have felt in my heart since the age of sixteen. I would have to add this chapter to my heart and close the door. It was my survival mode that I had taught myself in order to make it through the days. Just like I closed the door to the main part of the house as I entered into my apartment, I would once again hide from what I truly wanted to remember and leave those fond memories there.

I sat down on my bed and just listened to the silence for a moment. My parents had always believed in me…I just needed to finally believe in myself. The heck with living in the moment, focusing on myself and my future were now my priority. I knew what I had to do. I pulled out a suitcase from under my bed and threw in some clothes and toiletries. Then, I snuck threw the house again and into the garage. I grabbed my mom's old keys and was going to take her car that was still sitting there in the garage so that Stella wouldn't know I wasn't there. I rarely drove it so I was surprised it even started. I threw my stuff in the back seat and pulled out without my headlights on so that Stella wouldn't know. As I pulled out I saw my surfboard on the ground near my Jeep and grabbed it real quick to bring it with me just in case I decided to go surfing tomorrow. I already had my wetsuit so I might as well bring it with me too. I was going to drive to Cape May and get a hotel room. I had mentally started to plan my escape. I needed to clear my head and decide once and for all what my future held for me. I texted Ron Johnson on the way and he responded back right away. He was the one who ran the Cape May Beach and Wildlife Preservation Association. He said he would meet with me for breakfast tomorrow morning. He probably thought I was crazy for texting him at almost midnight. My phone was buzzing like crazy with text messages from Mel and Mercer but I couldn't bring myself to read them right now. I hopped on the Parkway and was on my way....

Brad's car pulled up in front of the Wright house shortly after midnight. He knew he had to win Summer over. He wasn't about to let her slip through his fingers. He knew she was worth millions and had every intention of ensuring he got his hands on the money someday. Brad had first seen Summer here and there around Mercer and did some digging to find out everything he could about her. He was attracted to her beauty but ultimately he wanted to ensure he found someone with money. He wanted to make sure he was financially secure and it would be a perk that she was hot too. He didn't care about love. He really just cared about himself. Brad saw Summer's car in the driveway and climbed the stairs and started knocking. She wasn't answering so he found her spare key that was hidden inside a shell and went inside. No one was there. Where could she be? He went back out to his car when Mercer drove up with Marnie. Mel had texted Mercer that Summer took off after seeing Chase kissing Amy.

"Well, well...look who it is" said Brad. "Where the hell is Summer?" said Mercer.
"Why do you care so much? You have a crush on her"? said Brad sharply.
"I know you are only with Summer for her money. You always hook up with girls as we both know and I heard you and your buddy joke about the money tonight. She has been through a lot and doesn't need you in her life to cause her more grief" said Mercer.

Brad glanced at his phone. Amy had just texted Brad and told him that Summer had hooked up with Chase with a passionate kiss and they were all over each other earlier. (She had x-ray eyes after all)...

"I think I know what's going on here" said Brad.

Brad hopped in the car and left to find Chase. He wanted to confront Chase and fight him. Chase had always been the obstacle with Summer. He knew deep down their connection was more than best friends. He wasn't an idiot. Mercer thought "good riddance" as Brad left and he ran up the stairs and couldn't find Summer anywhere. Her car was here but she wasn't home. It seemed odd. He ran over to Stella's to see if she was there. Bobby, Ben, Barry and Buck greeted him at the front door. He knew Stella was up because he too had seen her peaking through the blinds in the window even though it was way too late to be bothering her.

"Sorry to bother you Stella – is Summer here?
I can't find her and am worried about her" said Mercer.
"She got home almost an hour ago. I saw her
climb up the stairs and go inside
but she never came out" said Stella worried.
"I am sure she is around Stella, don't worry
about her. She just left the club early
after something happened with Chase and I was worried she was upset.
I am sure she is fine" Mercer assured Stella as Stella
couldn't help but think what an idiot Chase must be if he
didn't see all the wonderful things about Summer.

Mercer tried calling Summer as he walked down Stella's front steps but she didn't answer. He felt bad for worrying Stella. Mercer ran back into Summer's apartment and broke Summer's rule and went into the main part of the house but he couldn't find her. He had thought for sure that she was hiding somewhere in the house but not that he could see anyway. As he walked back outside and into Summer's driveway to get back to Marnie he noticed one important piece of Summer's décor was missing her new surf board.

"Oh my God" he said aloud. "She wouldn't do that, would she?"
Marnie walked up from waiting in the car. "Do what Mercer?"

In the meantime, Chase, Mel and Ronnie were on the trolley and had left the club. Mercer had texted them earlier that he couldn't find Summer and Brad was at the house looking for her too and had just left so he was checking at Stella's. Chase had already told Mel and Ronnie that Amy had kissed him and he pushed her away moments after it happened and Ronnie had witnessed it and could confirm. Chase confessed to them that he loved Summer. He wanted to tell her tonight and finally had the courage to tell her that and some other news when it all blew up in his face. Mel was so relieved. She knew how thrilled Summer would be. It would be so nice to see Summer so happy for once. She had dealt with enough. She had texted Summer but she didn't respond. Mercer had also texted Mel that Brad was after Summer for her money. Mel told Chase. Chase fumed with anger.

"Brad is such an asshole" yelled Chase. "I want to punch him the face. "I really thought Summer left with him when I saw them walk by" Chase finished infuriated.
"No way!" shared Mel. "Summer walked him to the door because he was kicked out. She just walked him outside to dump his ass" Mel said delightedly "she had planned on doing that for a while now and before we even went to the club she told me it was happening tonight".

Chase's anger quickly turned to relief. He couldn't bear losing Summer. She was everything to him. He told Mel and Ronnie he always loved her but never had the courage to tell her. Chase sat between Mel and Ronnie. He was pretty drunk. He put his arm around both of them and hugged them.

"I just love you Summer" moaned Chase.
"We aren't Summer, Chase, but we believe you" said Ronnie.
Mel rolled her eyes and laughed a little. "You two drive me crazy" she laughed thinking of Summer and Chase and all their drama.

Ronnie and Mel jumped off the trolley in front of the donut shop. Chase wanted to sober up a little before he faced Summer so he joined them. He was really wasted from doing those extra shots. They walked inside the shop. Mel and Ronnie went into the kitchen to make coffee for him to sober him up. Chase looked out the window and leaned his head against the glass. "Why did I wait so long" he thought to himself. He thought of his father's words to him last summer – "if you wait too long, you'll lose her". He couldn't let that happen. He reached for his phone and texted Mercer for an update on Summer. Chase couldn't ever let Summer slip through his fingers. He was tired of being afraid. What was the worst that could happen? She didn't feel the same way? At least he would know once and for all. He knew the kiss they shared was more than a kiss. It was two people in love with each other. He just hoped and prayed he was right.

Meanwhile, Brad was driving up and down the streets looking for the trolley to find Chase. John had told him he saw Chase leave. Brad drove by the donut shop and saw Chase in the window. "Now I got ya" thought Brad. He pulled over and wanted to confront him for making a move on his woman. Brad noticed that Chase seemed to be alone and thought of the perfect idea to keep him away long enough from Summer to win her back without his interference. He walked into the shop with a sly grin.

"We aren't open and you are not welcome you fucking asshole" said Chase.
"I know" said Brad, *"Why so harsh Chase?*
I was just thinking we could talk".

Before Chase could respond Brad grabbed Chase and they struggled. Chase was pretty drunk so he was no match for Brad but he still fought hard. Brad told Chase Summer would never like him as anything but a friend and he knocked Chase to the ground and pushed Chase into the Boogey Man closet and locked the door. Chase was too drunk to really have the strength to fight him. Summer had told Brad the story of how Mel's dad got locked in there. Chase knew he was screwed because Mel and Ronnie would just think he left and couldn't hear him. And to top it off, his phone had no reception in this stupid closet. Brad quickly left and hopped into his car and was going to head back to Summer's house to find her before Chase could get to her. And, from the way things looked, he would be locked in there all night until they opened in the morning.

In the meantime, Mercer was frantic thinking about the possibility of Summer night surfing alone. He needed to run home to get his board to find Summer. Surfer Girl, Marnie, came with him and said she would grab a board too and one of Mercer's old rash guards. He didn't want to go out there alone and take any chances. What he didn't realize was Summer wasn't night surfing at all. She had gone to Cape May. Mercer texted Chase with his fear that Summer went night surfing. He was sure Chase would show up any minute to help look for Summer. Mercer sped to his house and grabbed his board and another board for Marnie and one of his old rash guards. They raced back to Summer's house and headed out towards the sand.

"I hope she is o.k. It's so cloudy out. The moon doesn't even help light anything up out there" said Marnie.
"Chase will never live with himself if something happens to Summer" said Mercer.
"You are a terrific guy Mercer. You are a caring friend and not to mention – smoking hot" said Marnie with a smile. Mercer gave Marnie a hug and said *"you are right…about it all"*.
"Stuck up boy!" yelled Marnie as they both laughed.

They were both trying to lighten the mood and avoid the fact that Summer might be in trouble. The truth is though that they were both scared out of their mind. As they got up onto the beach and walked on the sand towards the water, their mood quickly changed as they looked out towards the dark ocean.

Chapter 10

My Escape

I pulled my Mom's old Mercedes Benz G-Class SUV, silver in color of course, into the Holiday Inn hotel parking lot and checked myself in. I was just glad they actually had vacancy and took me in. I had thrown my clothes and belongings into a suitcase without even thinking about what I was bringing. I didn't have pajamas and was still wearing my wet suit over my dress. I guess I did things kind of hastily and ran away. I didn't care though. My life felt like it was over as I had known it. Just like my life ended at sixteen when my parents died, it was now ending again for I would never have Chase. At least, not in the way I wanted to have him. I sounded dramatic but I really felt that way. My heart was aching. I texted Mel and told her I was fine and went to Cape May to the Holiday Inn and was going to talk to Ron over breakfast about taking him up on his offer for the job there and that I needed a change. I could see I had several messages but just couldn't read them right now. I turned my phone off and didn't even give her a chance to respond to me. I didn't want to be bothered for the night. Mel knew I was safe so there was nothing else I had to worry about. Stella thought I was sound asleep. I certainly wasn't going to tell Chase where I was. He was probably using my apartment to hook up with Amy anyway. He made me sick.

I thought about what Robert had said to me about Chase telling him to stay away from me. Why would Chase do that to me? Didn't he ever want me to meet someone? If he really loved me, why hadn't he told me ever over the twenty-one years I had known him. Could there still be a chance for us? I tried to stop my mind from thinking and to try and fall asleep. Nothing with Chase makes sense. My problems would still be there tomorrow so I might as well try and forget about them for the night I told myself. Plus, I wanted a clear mind to meet with Ron. I wanted to make sure I was making the right decision by turning down the aquarium role and moving to Cape May to work for Ron. Maybe it was the change I needed….or, the biggest mistake I could make. Life is like that. One door opens and takes you down a different path. You never really know if the path you chose is the right one.

Back in Avon-by-the-Sea, Marnie and Mercer ran up to the edge of the water with their boards.

> *"This is weird", Mercer told Marnie, "Summer always lays her stuff on the sand and there's nothing around".*

They went out into the water tumbling in the waves and finally making it to calmer water but didn't see her anywhere.

> *"I'm totally freaking out Mercer. It is pitch black out here. I can't see anything. Maybe we should call the coast guard?!" said Marnie.*

Mercer knew she was right. Summer could be in serious trouble or drifted too far out. Plus, they were putting themselves at risk too being out there. They made it back onto the shore. Marnie tumbled as she came in.

> *"You are hot when you're clumsy" said Mercer.*

"You are right, I am" said Marnie laughing. *"I just can't see a damn thing and other than your rash guard, I am wearing the shorts I wore to the club so it's not exactly surfing attire!"*

They grabbed their towels on the beach and dried themselves off. They walked off the beach and back up to Summer's house. Brad was there again.

"Jesus Christ!" muttered Mercer to Marnie displeased.
"This guy won't quit" agreed Marnie.
"I know that Chase kissed Summer tonight. I took care of him and now I am going to take care of you" screamed Brad as he approached Mercer and Marnie.
"Back off dude. Summer is missing. We think she went night surfing and may have drifted out too far" said Mercer concerned.

Brad's mood quickly changed. If something happened to Summer, he would never get his hands on her money.

"Let's check one more time in the house and try texting her and if we can't find her, we'll call the coast guard" said Marnie.

Marnie, Mercer and Brad went into Summer's apartment. Mercer could see Stella looking at the window and he gave her a thumbs up. He felt so bad for lying but he didn't want Stella to worry. Stella would assume they were all just hanging out. They went through Summer's apartment to the entryway into the main part of the house and looked everywhere. Mercer wondered where the heck Chase was. Why wasn't he here looking for Summer and what did Brad mean he had "taken care of him"? Maybe Chase already had found her and Brad was playing games. He couldn't worry about Chase right now. He had to find Summer and make sure she was o.k. first.

Marnie walked in the lower level of the house calling for Summer. She looked up in the dining room and noticed the beautiful chandelier full of shells and sea glass. She didn't know anything about Summer except that this house was gorgeous and that she hoped that Chase and Summer could work things out. Brad walked through the kitchen and decided to open the door to the garage in case she was hiding in there. He peaked into the garage and noticed Summer's Mom's car was gone.

"Shit, she took her mother's car. She's not here" said Brad frustrated.

Mercer and Marnie peaked into the garage to confirm. Mercer texted Summer frantically and Chase too. Neither Chase nor Summer responded to him. Where was everyone? Mercer got a text from Mel telling him to come to the donut shop first thing in the morning and that Chase had taken off home because he was wasted. She knew where Summer was and she was safe. He read it aloud to Marnie. Probably not the smartest move with Brad listening in. Brad knew Mel wouldn't respond to a call from him. She always had Summer's back. He was forced to go along with the plan and meet with them in the morning.

Back in Cape May, I looked around my hotel room. I felt more lonely here than ever. Even being alone in my parent's large house, it was still home. I wondered if Cape May would just make me feel more alone. I was glad I hadn't gone night surfing alone. Robert calling me was like a guardian angel. I knew I could be in serious trouble if something happened and I was out there alone. Plus, Mercer and Chase would kill me if I did it and I knew it was risky and unsafe to go alone. My eyes had been shut for hours but my mind was still awake. It was now 2:00 a.m. I reached over and set my alarm clock for 7:00 a.m. I was meeting Ron at 8:30 a.m. for breakfast. I was so exhausted and finally, I fell asleep. It was a solid sleep too. I was mentally exhausted and needed it.

At 7:00 a.m., my alarm clock went off and I got up. I looked around the room and I remembered where I was. Too bad it wasn't a nightmare I thought. I took a hot shower and got dressed. I truly hoped I was making the right decision by taking this job. I wanted to honor my father's work and this was so important to him. I wanted my parents to be proud of me. My heart was in the aquarium but my head was in the fundraising state of mind. Plus, I needed to get away from Chase and start over. He was so involved in my life and I didn't want to lose him but I needed to get over him in the way that I had hoped to be with him. I needed to learn to let that go and being apart was the only way to do it. Chase didn't even have to know how I felt about him. Why bother. I never got to say goodbye to my parents. I was just forced to get on with life. I needed to treat my feelings for Chase the same way or so I told myself.

Mel and Ronnie were up early. They hadn't really even slept anyway. They headed downstairs from the apartment and into the donut shop. It was about 7:00 a.m. and the shop opened at 7:30 a.m. anyway.

"I just can't figure out where Chase went last night" said Mel.
"He was really drunk. I think he probably went to find Summer and probably is passed out in her bed waiting for her to come home" said Ronnie.

Summer still wasn't answering any of Mel's text messages and her phone was definitely off. Chase's phone seemed to be off too. At least Summer was safe but she didn't want her to take that job. She wanted them to work together at the aquarium like they had always planned. Ronnie was hired there too. It was supposed to be "their" plan - the new three musketeers. Where had all this come from? Summer had never even considered Ron's offer before. She was so happy at the aquarium. But, she also couldn't imagine what Summer was going through plus Summer didn't know Chase felt the same way....yet. Either way, she just didn't want Summer to make an emotional decision that she would regret.

Mel's parents came into the donut shop and started opening up. Mercer texted that "they" were on their way over.

"I guess that means Marnie. Mercer seems to really have hit it off with her" laughed Ronnie.

Mel's parents began their morning routine of getting everything ready for opening. Mel unlocked the closet door to help her father and saw Chase fast asleep plopped onto the floor.

"Chase, oh my God!" screamed Mel.
"Brad came in here and pushed me in while you were in the kitchen making me coffee" he groaned. *"He is probably after Summer by now".*

Mel didn't have a chance to explain when Mercer, Marnie and…. no, that can't be but yes….BRAD walked in! Brad had waited in his car for Mercer to pull up so that he could get the latest information on Summer. Chase stood to his feet and went to punch Brad but Mercer held him back.

"Not now, Chase, it's Summer. She took off in her Mom's car with her surfboard…. we can't find her anywhere!" said Mercer.

Mel told them that Summer had texted her late last night that she went to Cape May and was staying at the Holiday Inn down there to meet with Ron in the morning for breakfast.

"She is probably going to take Ron up on his offer for that job. She saw Chase with Amy and it was the nail in the coffin" said Mel.
"I can't get through to her because her cell phone is off" Mel continued.
"Why would she take her surf board?" asked Chase.
"She better not have broken our rule and gone out alone last night. I can't lose her when I finally almost have her".
Mercer grabbed Chase's arm…."where the hell did Brad go?" said Mercer.

They looked outside and sure enough his car was gone. He was going to beat Chase and get to Summer if it was the last thing he did. Brad had grabbed his grandmother's engagement ring from his apartment before he headed over to meet up with them this morning. He had wanted to ask Summer for her hand in marriage for her birthday in August but needed to get to her now and make sure his future was set. There was no way he was this close to making sure he had that money that he would let Chase mess it up for him. He knew he had to do something drastic.

Mercer drove Chase home. Chase couldn't worry about Brad. If Summer and him were meant to be, he had to trust that it would happen.

> "Thanks Dude. And, thanks Marnie. You are
> a cool chick" said Chase to Mercer
> and Marnie as they dropped him off and headed
> back to the donut shop for breakfast.

Chase took a quick shower and hopped in his truck and was headed to Cape May. He tried to call Summer but it went right to voice mail. He didn't leave a message. He stopped at a Wawa on the way that also happened to sell a bunch of souvenir-type stuff. He grabbed a large coffee and got the biggest conch shell he could find and a dozen pink roses. He grabbed a stationary set and a pen too and paid the cashier. Chase was horrible at expressing his feelings verbally so he decided to write it all down. As he drove down to Cape May, he thought about Summer. He thought about looking into her eyes last night and how it felt to have her in his arms. He thought about their amazing, passionate kiss. He just couldn't believe how incredible it felt to kiss her. He had news he was going to share with her too last night. He hoped he would have his chance and Brad wouldn't screw it up for him. He made it down to Cape May and pulled into the Holiday Inn Parking lot and saw that Summer's mom's car wasn't there. She was probably at breakfast with Ron and he had no idea where they were. He would wait. He grabbed a blanket from his trunk and walked up to the beach and wrote to Summer what he had always wanted to tell her trying to find the words he longed to share with her.

Brad was already at the Holiday Inn. He gave the front desk clerk a $20 bill to find out what room Summer was in and used his credit card to slide into the door crack to pop the door open and break into the room and waited for her. He had grabbed a few candles and lit them and put the ring in the middle. All he could do now was wait. Summer had no idea what was waiting for her when she returned. Brad wanted to beat Chase to the punch and hoped he was the one Summer wanted. She longed for family and he knew it. He would promise her a family life again and hopefully, she would be back under his spell if she was ever even under it in the first place.

Chase sat out staring at the ocean. How could he have let this harvest inside him for so long? There were so many times he wanted to tell Summer of his feelings for her but there was always something standing in his way…his fear, her parents' deaths, his immature ways in school of partying and hooking up….he would've screwed it up anyway if he had done it earlier and last night was supposed to be the perfect time to tell her. They were graduating now, and their futures were upon them. He wanted to start a life with Summer as a couple. He knew he loved her in that way. He wanted to marry her and have a family with her and never be without her. She had always been his world but now she was his whole world. Chase tried to find the words to write his letter. Why couldn't he be better at expressing his emotions? Maybe he wouldn't be in this situation if he had just told her when he had so many chances to do it. He put the pen on the paper and the words were simple and to the point. They came out easily and it wasn't at all hard like he thought it would be. He folded the paper and stuck it inside an envelope and wrote Summer on the outside of it. Now, like Brad, all he could do was wait for her to return. Neither Brad nor Chase knew of each other's plans. Both would simply wait for the girl of their dreams to return. It was the turning point both had been waiting for. Chase lay down on the sand and closed his eyes and waited.

Back in Avon by the Sea, Mel and Ronnie went up to the beach with Mercèr and Marnie with a bag of donuts and some coffees.

Mel placed a blanket on the sand and the four sat on the blanket and ate their breakfast. It was a little chilly and Mercer gave Marnie his hoodie to put on. All four wondered what the outcome would be of everything that had transpired.

> "My whole life I have watched Chase make one
> hundred percent sure that no guys
> ever went near Summer. He has always been in love with her but was
> always too chicken to tell her" said Mercer.
> "I agree" said Mel…"On the same note, Summer would never allow
> anyone to be as close to her as Chase was.
> Chase has always been Summer's whole world.
> She never even told me about
> you guys night surfing. She liked to have some sacred
> things between just her and Chase".
> "I just worry about Summer. I want them to have that ultimate happy
> ending. It would definitely turn Summer's life around and fill a lot
> of the void she has felt for so long without her Mom and Dad"
> chimed in Ronnie.

Marnie listened. She didn't even know that Summer's parents were gone. She felt an overwhelming sadness. It made more sense now why Summer took off. She didn't blame her. She couldn't imagine what she had been going through. Marnie was new to this group but so glad she was there. It felt like she had known these people forever and it hasn't even been a day. Mercer was the ultimate catch for her and she hoped he could love her someday the way Chase and Summer seemed to love each other. They all sat there on the beach with their phones in hand.

> "We look pathetic" laughed Mel as they all sat there staring at
> their phones anxiously awaiting word from Summer or Chase.

They all started to laugh as they ate the donuts and coffee.

Chapter 11

A Ring, A Letter and A Promise

I arrived at the Victorian Sea Inn about thirty minutes early so that I would have time alone to reflect until Ron got there. I hadn't been there since that fateful night when I lost my parents. I walked up onto the beautiful porch covered in sunlight and thought about how beautiful my Mom had looked that terrible 4th of July night. I thought about her words about how "important these events were". I hoped I was making the right job choice. I wanted them to be proud of my choices. I wished they were here to tell me what to do and guide me. I chose a small table outside so that I could look out at the ocean. Cape May truly was a beautiful area I thought as I looked around. I could be happy here, couldn't I? The ocean is still here, the sand, the marine life, the beaches…it's just the people that aren't. But it's not like I would be moving to another State…it's just a few hours away. That's not so bad. Ron pulled up about fifteen minutes later and I watched him get out of his car and walk up towards the Inn. He looked just the same as I remembered him. He had always stayed in touch with me through the years but I haven't seen him since the funeral in person. He had jeans and a bottom up white shirt. He was a handsome black man who was also very tall and in my opinion looked like an NBA basketball player. He came up onto the porch and saw me. He came right over with a huge smile and gave me a hug and told me I looked just like my mother. It was true and it meant a lot to hear it from someone else.

"Summer, I am so glad you are here" said Ron
and he gave me a kiss and a hug.
"You are a spitting image of your mom Summer" shared Ron.
"Thank you Ron. You are too kind" I told him.

For some reason, my heart just started to pound in my chest. I hugged him really hard and probably too long. I think I was just emotionally drained. We sat down at the table. A waitress came and we put in our orders.

"So, I got your text" said Ron.
"Yes" I replied.

It was awkwardly quiet and I looked down at my coffee and Ron could tell I was struggling with the words.

"Tell me the real reason you are here" Ron said.

I looked Ron in the eyes and that's when it all came out....I decided not to hold anything in and filled him in on all that had transpired. Poor guy must have thought – "what am I getting myself into?!". I told him how important the marine animals were to me. I told him about Chase, Brad and even Robert. I told him about the camp program and all I had done with it and how important the kids were to me. Everything just sort of poured out. I wanted him to know the whole story so he could help me and understand where I was coming from. Ron sat there calmly and listened. When I was done, I was emotionally drained. I hadn't even noticed my breakfast was served and Ron had almost eaten his entire plate. He just sat there with a smile.

> "You are smiling?" I said to Ron.
> "Yes" said Ron, as if it was like he already knew
> the whole story and had all the answers.
> "I think I know what we can do to give you the
> best of both worlds" he said confidently.

Ron filled me in on his plan. Ron told me that a few years ago he purchased the Aquarium as a silent partner as a part of expanding his foundation and fundraising reach. He told me he just closed the deal with a Finance Manager and hired them to work out of the aquarium and be responsible for the events and fundraising.

> "The best part is that you can be a key partner in these events
> but as an extension of your role at the aquarium. This way
> you can get involved and help me out and work directly with
> the Finance Manager there without having to give up your
> day job working with the animals and camp programs".

For once in this dreadful weekend, I finally had an answer to something and his plan was perfect. It was everything I always wanted. I knew Ron was going to figure it out for me somehow. I only wished I had the confidence to sit there and smile when someone tells me their troubles. Robert did the same thing. It was like they were in on some secret that I didn't know about.

> "This is the perfect solution for me Ron. I have been struggling with
> honoring what was so important to my parents and yet needed to focus
> on what I love as well and this really is the best of both worlds. Plus, I
> can stay in Avon-by-the-Sea. I will have to face Chase eventually and
> in my heart, I never really wanted to leave. I was just running away".

I hugged him as we were going to our cars. I felt like Ron already knew everything I had told him. It was almost like he was there with me through it all. As I got into my car, he told me to follow my heart and that I should give Chase a chance to explain.

"Love doesn't always work the way you want it to but in the end it always finds a way Summer. Just follow your heart. Trust that you know what's best for you in your heart and it will all work out. I promise" smiled Ron.

We said good-bye and I sat in my car. I thought about what Ron had said and he was right. I needed to follow my heart more often. I didn't know what would happen with Chase but I couldn't run away from everything. I needed to face him eventually. I could only hope that I could salvage some type of relationship with him. Even if we didn't end up together and he wanted Amy after all, I would need to learn to live with it. Chase was too important to just let everything we have shared go out the window. Ron's words and plans were perfect in this moment. I didn't have a parent to go to for advice. I needed an adult to count on and I guess I needed to remember I was an adult now too. Free to make choices that I could count on and follow my own heart.

I pulled away from the Inn and headed back towards the hotel feeling pretty good but tired. I turned into the Holiday Inn parking lot and headed into the building. I just wanted to get my stuff and get ready to check out. I needed to talk to Chase and get the whole story from him. I turned my phone on in the elevator and read through some of my texts from Mel and Mercer….none from Chase. I got to the one about Brad being after me for my money from Mercer. This is why he had punched him. I guess I should have known. Not that it really surprised me at all. The funny part was I didn't even really care. I didn't want anything to do with him anymore anyway. I made it to my room and put the key-card into the door and entered. As I lay my purse and phone on the bed, I saw something flickering and noticed the lit candles surrounding a ring box.

"What's going on?" I asked aloud.

To my surprise, Brad came out from hiding on the side of the bed and startled me.

"Summer, I can't let you go that easily. We have been together on and off for a few years and I love you. I want to start a family and life with you. The family you lost can look down and see you happy and a part of a new family. Please, will you be my wife?" Brad pleaded and got on one knee and grabbed the ring box and removed the ring.

He handed me the ring. I was in a daze.

"How did you get in here? What are you doing here?" was all I managed to get out.
Brad told me *"I broke in but I had too. I have always wanted you to be with me forever and I can't let you slip away from me"*.
"I think you should just leave Brad. We broke up last night remember?" I managed to get out handing him back the ring from my hand.
"Besides Mercer texted me and told me you are after my money. I should've have figured it out a long time ago because no one in their right mind would've let me string them along for so many years without pushing for more. I really don't ever want to see you again" I told Brad as I pushed him away and blew out the candles and pushed him again towards the door.
"It's not true Summer. It started out that way. I come from nothing and I wanted to have everything but I really do love you" pleaded Brad.
"Then, I am really sorry if that is true. Maybe in the future you should have the best intentions from the very beginning when you are with someone, but that person in your future will not be me" I told him.

I pushed him through the door and stood in the doorway. He didn't really even try and argue. I think deep down he knew he was wrong. As he walked away, he told me to enjoy my lonely life and that Chase and Amy were together and I was the loser that would end up alone. I just shut the door and rolled my eyes. I took a deep breath and bolted the door locked just in case. I should've known better about Brad. What a waste of time and life is too short to waste time on things that you know aren't what you want. It was nice to finally have that clarity at least.

I grabbed my phone off the bed and texted Mel - "I have news that you will be happy with – on my way back and will call you when I get there. Tell Mercer thank you. Haven't heard from Chase". I started to pack up my stuff so that I could get out of here. I couldn't believe I just got proposed to but it was definitely from the wrong guy. Mel was right; I should of dumped his ass years ago. I threw my clothes and toiletries back into my bag. I wanted to go home. For the first time in a long time, it really felt like "home" and it was slowly becoming "my home". Maybe I would even venture into the house part of my home. It's been too long and it would be nice to finally bring some of that house back to life. I felt like my parents would be happy that I made a job choice that made me happy and did a little bit of both of the things I like to do. I waited a few minutes to make sure Brad would be gone and then I would head down to the lobby and check out.

Outside, Brad walked off the elevator with the ring in one hand and the ring box and his car keys in the other. He was pissed that he had come so close to getting what he wanted only to fail. He would have to find someone else to target. There was no way he was going to struggle his whole life and live the way he grew up. Brad exited the elevator and walked past the lobby front desk and towards the doors to leave the hotel lobby. At the same time Chase walked towards the doors into the lobby. There they were face to face.

"You are too late Chase. I asked Summer to marry me and she said yes" bragged Brad.
He showed him the empty box while hiding the ring in his other hand and said "the ring is on Summer's finger and I am headed out to get some champagne for the two of us and we are going to celebrate...in bed."

Chase couldn't believe it. He didn't say anything and just watched Brad walk to his car. He watched Brad pull away and out of the parking lot. "How could Summer be so blind? Had she really given up on me completely?" thought Chase. He had the letter, flowers and shell in his bag and was contemplating what to do when he saw Summer get off the elevator and walk over to the front desk with all her stuff.

"I'd like to check out" I told the front desk.

Chase ran outside to be unnoticed. It wouldn't surprise him if Brad had lied but he didn't know for sure. He had saw Brad pull out and head out onto the highway so it didn't seem like he was running locally to get champagne. He snuck over to Summer's mom's car quickly while she was checking out and placed the letter inside the conch shell on top of Summer's mom's car and hid behind another car praying and was hopeful it would work out. He saw Summer walking over to the car through the parking lot. "This could be it" thought Chase. "It's finally my chance and I can't screw this up"…..

I threw my stuff in the trunk of my mom's car and went to hop in when I noticed a gigantic shell and a letter that said "Summer" on the envelope. My first reaction was that I really didn't care what Brad had to say but I noticed my name wasn't written in his hand-writing. I also knew Brad wouldn't be thoughtful enough to take the time to get a shell for me. I reached up and grabbed the shell and letter and looked at it for a moment. I would recognize that hand-writing anywhere. I pulled out the letter and put the shell on my front seat. I looked around but didn't see Chase anywhere. I was so excited and also so scared to read this letter. I shut the car door and grabbed my surf board out of the trunk and walked up to the beach and lay down my surf board on the sand to sit on it and read the letter. I took a deep breath and began to read…

Summer:

Like a typical boy likes girl, I tortured you when we were younger a lot but it was "because I love you".
I often pushed you in the pool and try to embarrass you in front of guys "because I love you".
I call and text you every day "because I love you".
I snuggle with you and sleep over "because I love you".
I was there for you before and after your parents became angels "because I love you".
I have never had a serious girlfriend "because I love you".
I kissed you last night in the bar not because of Amy but "because I love you".
I pushed Amy away when she tried to kiss me last night "because I love you".

I have always loved you. Not because we grew up together, not because we are best friends and not because you lost your parents. Because you are beautiful – inside and out. You make me want to be a better person. Because I can't live without you and will never not have you in my life in one way or another.

I am horrible with words and it took me hours just to write these few words but I did it "because I love you". I know you love me too but I want you to love me in the "I want to spend my life with you" kind of way because that is how I love you.

XOXO
Chase

My hand covered my mouth and tears rolled down my face as I sat up and looked out at the ocean. I clutched the letter against my chest and cried. Cape May had brought so much loss to me yet now it was giving something back to me - my one true love, Chase.

"I can't believe it" I said aloud.

I saw a shadow in the sand of a man appear next to me. I turned to see Chase holding pink roses.

"Chase!" I said.
"Don't speak!" said Chase firmly as he kneeled down next to me.
"I know you are marrying Brad. He showed me the empty
ring box but I still had to still give you the letter."

I went to respond to tell Chase he was wrong but Chase put his finger over my lips so that I couldn't speak.

Chase continued "Wait. Let me finish. I was always to chicken
to tell you and I can't live with myself knowing I didn't at
least try. I love you Summer. I always have and I don't ever
want to lose you" Chase said with his voice shaking.
"You have always been the love of my life. I have wanted to tell you for
years" said Chase relieved to have finally revealed his true feelings.

I grabbed Chase's hand and looked at him full of exhilaration and relief.

"I would never EVER marry Brad, Chase. I broke up with him
last night before any of this happened. I've also realized that I would
never move to Cape May. I would never let you go if you love me in
the – I want to spend my life with you – kind of way.... because like
you said in your letter, it's because I too love you" I told Chase.
"I have loved you my whole life too and can't imagine
being with anyone but you" I said with bliss.

I couldn't believe I finally said it after holding it in my whole life.

*"You love me too in the "I want to spend my life with
you kind of way"?" said Chase making sure.
"Yes, I do" I responded with tears streaming down my face and
Chase grabbed me and hugged me laying on top of me and rolling
me off my board and onto the sand making us both laugh.
"God, I love you so much Summer" Chase said with
tears in his eyes and he leaned in and kissed me.*

It felt so good to kiss him again. I was still crying and now Chase was too. It wasn't tears of sadness but of happiness for Chase in my life. I couldn't imagine being with someone else ever. We kissed each other so hard and intensely again. I never wanted to kiss anyone ever again. He held me so tightly and I could feel the passion in his embrace was as strong as mine. We managed to sit back up on my board and dust the sand off of us and I wrapped my legs around him facing him and he pulled me close.

*"Things worked out with Ron?" Chase asked as we sat back
up and were both sitting on my board looking at each other.
"Yes, he came up with a plan" I told Chase happily
as he wiped my tears from my eyes.
"I can't believe it....I can stay in Avon-by-the-Sea
but still be able to help out his foundation".
"I know" said Chase as he grabbed my hands and intertwined them
with his and pulled me even closer to him. "You do?" I asked. "He also
offered me a job to run the finances for his fundraising efforts a few days
ago but not in Cape May. We've been talking for months actually.
Ron bought ownership in the Aquarium about two years ago. I
will be working in the aquarium offices but working for Ron as
their finance manager. I love finance but I missed the aquarium too
and wanted to find a way to merge the two. I reached out to Ron*

about six months ago and we finally were able to work something out. I wanted to tell you last night…among other things".

No wonder Ron seemed "clued in". Ron had agreed that I take the job at the aquarium where I really wanted to be and instead, he wanted to start partnering with the aquarium to co-sponsor events to raise money for the beaches and marine life on the Jersey Coast under his new financial manager who would office out of the aquarium's offices. It would allow me to do what I loved and still do something important, more importantly something important to my parents. I could make them proud and myself happy all in one. Ron left out the financial manager's name that I would be working with – it was Chase. No wonder Ron had smiled. He did know. Everything was finally coming together in my life and all the pieces finally fitting together. Chase truly was the glue that held me together and I was his glue. I melted into Chase's arms and whispered to him.

"I can't imagine being happier in any moment than the one I am in right now with you. You really are everything to me and I can't believe it will be you that I will be working with too. I am so happy" I told Chase hugging him and Chase pulled me close and we were both aching for each other physically.

Both of our breathing was fast and short and it was agonizing how badly we wanted each other as we kissed and embraced each other. It was such a tender and raw moment. We both wanted each other so badly. I could feel him pushing and rubbing into me as my legs were wrapped around him and I ached so badly for him. He kissed my neck and my lips. I could feel him thrusting into me and it made me ache for him and I could feel him throbbing for me too.

"It's too bad you already checked out of the Holiday Inn" teased Chase as he ran his hands down my back to my waist and pressed against me as wanting each other was excruciating.

We both smiled and were amused at his comment and he kissed me passionately again and our hands were all over each other. I had found my happy ending at last.

"I can't believe I have found what my parents had and it had been right in front of me my whole life" I told Chase. "I've always known Summer. Always." whispered Chase as we hugged each other.
"I have too. I was just afraid you wouldn't feel
the same way" I said to Chase softly.
"Me too" shared Chase. "My biggest fear was that you just wanted me because I had so much loss and you didn't want to let me down too. I wanted you to want me for being me and not because it was to make up for my losses". Chase cupped my face with his hands and looked at me deeply into my eyes. I felt like he could almost touch my soul. "You have had such tremendous loss Summer but I love you and only you. The things that have happened are not what I ever would want for you or anyone but they have nothing to do with how I feel about you. I felt this way when your parents were here and still feel the same way without them here. Don't EVER think that. I just love YOU. Plain and simple." I hugged him again and we just stayed there for a few minutes in an embrace.

Chase and I did indeed go back into the Holiday Inn. I told the front desk I forgot something in the room and luckily they hadn't deactivated my key card yet and we went up together. In the elevator on the way up, I told him I wanted to "seal the deal" to steal his line from the night before and he laughed and kissed me. As we rode up the elevator, he leaned over me pushing me against the wall and looked at my body.

"Summer…I want you so, so bad. You have
NO idea" said Chase passionately.
"I've never wanted anyone like I want you Chase" I told him.

We barely made it into the room and we were pulling each other's clothes off. He threw off my clothes and stripped me down to my bra and underwear and kissed me while I pulled off his shirt and tried to undo his pants. He unhooked my bra and leaned down and kissed my breasts as I pulled at his belt on his pants and undressed him. He caressed my breasts and couldn't stop telling me how beautiful I was. He slid down my undies and touched me and kissed me. I touched him and kissed him too and he sighed with pleasure. He lifted me on the bed and we started to make love. It was so amazing and I just couldn't believe we had waited this long to be together. We were so attracted to each other and neither of us has ever wanted someone more. Being with him and knowing he would be the last man I would ever be intimate with was so satisfying. I really did have it all because I had him and I knew he felt the same way about me. Chase kept whispering to me how sexy and beautiful I am. He kissed my entire body and I kissed and touched him until we were both ready to explode. He lay on top of me and went inside me. As soon as he entered I couldn't help but moan and sigh with pleasure and so did he. With each thrust my body shook in ways I have never experienced before and we stared into each other's eyes . We both came together and he exploded inside me. We both just stayed frozen in that moment and neither of us had the strength to open our eyes or even move. He finally kissed me passionately and we were both panting and out of breath and my eyes filled with tears. We were still throbbing inside each other. I told him how much I loved him and it felt amazing to hear him say it back to me.

As we straightened ourselves up in the bathroom to leave, Chase told me "obviously I have had sex before, but I have never made love with anyone until now".
"God, I love you so much Summer and you are the sexiest, most beautiful girl on this planet" and he hugged me tightly.
"I just want to do this again and again and again" I said kissing him.
"We are definitely on the same page baby" Chase responded while he kissed and hugged me.

I thought "could I be any luckier? I have the man of my dreams next to me". As we left through the lobby, the front desk clerk asked if we found what we were looking for. Chase and I looked at each other and both just smiled and said "yes, definitely yes".

Chase and I put our arms around each other as we walked out to the cars to follow each other back to Avon-by-the-Sea. When we got to his car, Chase told me to wait one minute and he reached into his glove compartment and handed me a necklace. It was the one my parents had given me as a child that said Summer. He had it all this time.

*"Where did you find this"? I asked Chase. "I
lost that necklace so many years ago".
"I've had it all this time Summer. I'm sorry. It
was a way for me to be close to you,
even when we weren't together. I'm sorry I never told you" responded Chase.*

I kissed him before he could even say anything else. He really had felt the same way his whole life. This was confirmation for me. It was important for me to know and trust that he wanted me and not because my parents had died but because he really had loved me his whole life. I lost the necklace a long time before I lost my parents so I knew even way back then, he was in love with me…just as I had always been in love with him. He truly was my other half. I let him keep the necklace. I didn't need it anymore. I had everything I wanted in the world, with the exception of my parents. He hung the necklace from his rearview mirror and it looked perfect there. I finally had my perfect soul mate and the empty space in my heart was full.

*"I guess we should head home and let the others know we are o.k." I said.
Chase responded with a wink "Unless you forgot
something else inside the Holiday Inn?"*

Chapter 12

A New Girl in Chase's Life

It was Christmas later that year and Chase and I had been officially together now for more than six months, although we had been together our whole lives in one way or another too. I couldn't wait to see what he would get me for Christmas. He had pretty much moved into my small apartment and we were planning for our future in Avon-by-the-Sea. We started to clean out and renovate the main part of the house, although it was a difficult process for me. In the six years since my parents were killed, I hadn't even looked in their drawers or gone through their clothing. It was a lot to deal with but I had Chase by my side very step of the way. Even with all of that, I loved this house too much to sell it. I couldn't leave Stella either. She was getting older and it was my turn to look after her as she had done for me for so long. Brice was also in love and still with Marcella. Stella was so happy he had found someone true and non-Hollywood. Work was going well and it was so great to work not only with Chase but with Mel and Ronnie too. Mel and Ronnie were engaged to be married and had gotten engaged at the end of the summer. I was so happy for them and Chase and I had helped Ronnie surprise Mel with the proposal. We pulled a Chase and snuck into the aquarium at night and set up a picnic by the penguin tank for them. Mel hasn't stopped smiling since it happened. Mercer is doing great too and was teaching at the local high school and dating Marnie seriously. We all seemed to have life going in the right direction for ourselves. I even heard that Amy was dating Brad. They probably deserved each other and it made us all laugh at the thought of them together. Amy's parents were pretty well-off so it wouldn't surprise me if he had his next target.

Chase had told me to stay in bed that Christmas morning and to close my eyes while he went to get my gift. I peeked out the window and saw him run over to Stella's house. He must have hid my gift over there that sneak! I quickly hopped back in bed and closed my eyes. I could hear him walk into the room.

Chase said "open your eyes Summer" as he carried a large box and was holding it very carefully.

He laid it on the bed and I lifted off the lid excitedly. Inside was a tiny toy yorkie female puppy with a red bow.

"Oh my God!!!!! Chase!!!! She is so sweet!" I said as I picked up the puppy and kissed it adoringly.

I had wanted a yorkie for SO SO long! She reminded me of my little Buttercup and of Bobby.

"I wanted you forever little puppy. Thank you so much baby" I said kissing him and tears streaming down my cheeks.
"What should we name her Chase?"
"How about Rose since you love them so much?" suggested Chase.
"It is the perfect name. Come here Rosie my sweetheart" I said to the new puppy.
"Don't you notice something else on the puppy Summer?" asked Chase anxiously.

The red ribbon around Rose's neck had something hanging from it. It was a ring….an engagement ring to be exact.

"Oh my God, Chase!" I screamed.
Chase got down on one knee and smiled…"Summer, will
you do me the honor of marrying me and be my wife?"
"Yes, I will. I will!" I said with no hesitation and we
hugged and almost squeezed Rose too much.
"I can't believe this. I love you baby" I said to
Chase softly as he slipped the beautiful
diamond ring onto my finger and the tears rolled down my face.
"Not as much as I love you" said Chase "You
really are my world, Summer".
"And you are mine. You always have been and always will be.
You make me the happiest I could ever be just by loving me" I shared.
Chase gave me a kiss and yelled "Woo Hoo! You can come in now Stella".

Stella had been waiting outside the door anxiously. I ran and hugged Stella and we both cried. The ring was a rock not that I needed one and I couldn't stop staring at it. I knew Abbie had probably helped Chase pick it out and pay for it. It was easily 5 or 6 carats and a round simple solitaire. I loved it. I also absolutely loved this puppy. She was the cutest thing in the whole world. There was nothing like the unconditional love of a puppy. Their innocence and their pure happiness were contagious. Only dog people would understand what I mean. They just bring such joy to your life.

Chase and I had talked about getting married in the next year or two but I didn't think he had planned anything yet so he really surprised me. I didn't need the ring though. I just needed him. We didn't waste any time and put the plans in motion. We had wasted so much time through high school and college not being together when we should've been so getting married was not something we wanted to delay. Chase and I married that coming summer a few weeks apart from Mel and Ronnie. We didn't really bother to wait.

It was so fun that I got to go through it all with Mel. We were both trying on wedding gowns, going to cake tastings, checking out venues and we did it together every step of the way. Ronnie and Chase just let us handle it all like typical guys but they did enjoy the cake tasting. At my bridal shower, Abbie had put together a slide show of pictures of Chase & me through the years. It reminded us both that we really were together our whole lives and my parents were a big part of it which made me so happy. I wonder if deep down they knew Chase and I would end up together. The thought made me smile. The slideshow was so meaningful to me and of course Abbie had made another celebration so special for me. That summer, we married at a beautiful bed and breakfast in our town and said our vows on the beach. I couldn't imagine doing it anywhere else. Abbie had managed the whole ceremony and worked with a party planning company to make it beautiful. There were white folding chairs lined up into rows and a long white path way lined with candles and shells in the middle. Each end chair had beautiful pink roses tied to them, my favorite. The alter had an archway full of pink and white roses. She had baskets full of flip flops for guests to remove their shoes and walk comfortably on the sand.

Chase told me that before they walked out to the alter, Mercer had taken the groomsmen into a huddle like we did on our surfing spring break. He said "this is your final moment Chase; the moment you've been waiting for, and all of us have been waiting for too by the way, your whole life". Chase couldn't help but agree and laugh with Mercer. He had finally grown up. He had the woman of his dreams by his side and he couldn't wait to spend the rest of his life with her. She was his best friend, Chase's Summer finally.

Chase's father walked me down the aisle proudly. I knew my Dad wouldn't want it any other way than having his best friend be there for me in such a special moment. It was the perfect day minus having my parents there. I wore the most beautiful wedding gown. It was a Vera Wang gown with a strapless top and covered in Lace and the train was complete see-through lace that matched my veil.

It looked magnificent as it trailed behind me. I pinned an angel pin that I found in my mom's jewelry box that had a blue stone in it that was my mother's inside the bottom of the dress. Something borrowed and something blue and I knew my mom would love that. I knew my parents were smiling down on me. Abbie and Sam couldn't have been prouder. They told me they were waiting a long time for this to happen. Chase & I had been waiting a long time too. Ryan, Mercer and Ronnie were our groomsmen and Mel, Stella and one of Chase's cousins that I had known from growing up, Camille, were my bridesmaids. Stella carried Rose down the aisle too and Rose had a small pink rose barrette in her fur on top of her head. Abbie really thought of it all! We got married in the summer because it is our favorite time of year. Chase and I wrote our own vows and didn't share them with each other in advance. Chase pulled out the letter he had written to me on the beach in Cape May that day and read it to me but changed the end and deleted the last paragraph and told me I've made his dreams come true and how much he can't wait to spend the rest of his life with me by my side. I told Chase he was the love of my life, my whole life. Down the shore, you often saw planes fly by pulling banners with advertisements and announcements. I had a plane drive by and pointed to the sky during my vows and it said "Chase – I am marrying my best friend. I love you. –Summer" and the guests all clapped and Chase hugged me. Chase was always doing nice things and surprising me so I wanted to surprise him.

At the reception, Abbie had large centerpieces in the middle of each table in beautiful crystal vases with pink and white roses in them. Surrounding the bottom of each vase were shells and starfish. They looked so beautiful. I had picked out the perfect favors for our beach wedding. They were little boxes of chocolates in the shapes of starfish and shells. We also had cookies shaped like sand-dollars with white icing and starfish ones with blue icing attached to the box of chocolates. I attached my favorite poem on paper rolled and tied up in a ribbon to each box. The poem was actually a part of a speech given by President Kennedy that he had done in Newport, Rhode Island at an America's Cup dinner in 1962. For some reason, his words always stuck with me. The paper read:

> "I really don't know why it is that all of us are so committed to the sea, except I think it is because in addition to the fact that the sea changes and the light changes, and ships change, it is because we all came from the sea. And it is an interesting biological fact that all of us have, in our veins the exact same percentage of salt in our blood that exists in the ocean, and, therefore, we have salt in our blood, in our sweat, in our tears. We are tied to the ocean. And when we go back to the sea, whether it is to sail or to watch it we are going back from whence we came." – John F. Kennedy
>
> Thank you for celebrating with us and for sharing our love of the ocean.
> –Chase & Summer

These favors sat beautifully at each place setting. The poem also made me feel like my parents were there with me. I had released their ashes back into the ocean; back from whence they came. They were where they should be and it made them feel even more there for my wedding day. We had a DJ play since Chase and I liked to hear the real thing versus a band, although having The Nerds would've been a fun idea. We danced our first dance to "Lucky" by Jason Mraz and Colbie Caillat. The song was so perfect for us. It mentions the ocean, being with your best friend plus I was "lucky I was in love with my best friend and lucky to be coming home" like the song mentions. I didn't do a father/daughter dance but instead after Chase and I did our first dance, we stayed out there and Sam announced this dance was for Summer's parents. It was to Garth Brooks "The Dance". Everyone sobbed while we danced and so did I. It wasn't all sadness though it was just that I loved them so much. I sang along "I'm glad I didn't know the way it all would end, the way it all would go. Our lives are better left to chance. I could've missed the pain but I'd have had to miss the dance". It was the truth and how I would live my life now. Not in the past but in the present and enjoying every moment. It was the most painful and yet most beautiful moment of my life to honor my parents in that way in front of everyone we loved with Chase by my side. As the rest of the night went on, we knew exactly how we wanted to end this special day. We made sure the DJ played "Purple Rain" by Prince as the last song of the night. Mercer, Chase, Mel, Ronnie, Ryan, Marnie and I huddled in and sang it on the top of our lungs. It was another one of our moments together and I knew there were many more to come. It was the perfect ending to the perfect day. Chase and I went to Hawaii on our honeymoon and Stella gladly watched Rose for us.

Another even bigger milestone happened just two years later when we had a baby girl. We named her Carissa, after my mother. She was 6 lbs and 7 ounces and 19 ½ inches long. She was born in September. She was a combination of Chase and I and pure perfection. She had blonde hair and Chase's hazel green eyes. I would just stare at her all day long in amazement. Chase told me he never thought he could ever love another girl as much as he loved me until Carissa came along. She was the new girl in Chase's life. We were the three musketeers plus Rose. Mel and Ronnie had a baby boy about six months after us and named him Ronald Edward also known as Ronnie, Jr. They used my Dad's name as the middle name and it meant a lot to me. Mel and Ronnie had a bought a small house a few blocks from us. Chase and I were done remodeling my parent's house and we made it our own. We put in a new kitchen and hard wood floors throughout the home. We painted and put up molding. It looked like a different house. We were no longer in the little apartment but had brought the house back to life. Stella says she wouldn't even recognize the inside of our house if it weren't for that shell chandelier. That light will always stay with me and it still looks beautiful. When the sea glasses sparkles, it makes me think of my mom and that it's a sign from her that she is here with me. Stella gave me the picture she had drawn of Chase & I surfing when we were younger and I proudly displayed it in my living room.

I remember Mel came over one day and we were sitting in the porch with the babies. I remember seeing Carissa and Ronnie Jr. sitting in their carriages smiling at each other this day and thinking "oh boy, a new generation of trouble". I could only hope they would be life-long friends like Mel, Chase, Mercer and I were. Speaking of Mercer, Mercer and Marnie are engaged now. They are living in the area too in an apartment until they get married. They will eventually buy a house here. Both are still surfing all the time - not that it's a surprise. Mercer still has his surfing blog too. He said he couldn't wait for the day that Carissa would be his local surfer of the month. I don't think she'll have a choice. She will be surfing, at the beach and visiting the aquarium whether she wants to or not. But somehow, I think she will want to…it's in her blood to love the ocean.

I still work at the aquarium, although part-time now since Carissa has arrived, and love it. We have some new college interns working there with the camp program just as I did with Mel and Ronnie. There was one girl named Amber who had just started a few weeks ago. She was also new to the area. She was thinking of moving down to Avon-by-the-Sea after graduation from North Jersey and working full-time at the aquarium. She once asked me why I chose to live in Avon-by-the-Sea and I told her as I smiled and said my Dad's words aloud – **"for the love of the ocean"**.

About the Author

Christine Lynn Lourenco earned a Bachelor of Arts degree in Communication Studies from Montclair State University. When she is not writing, Christine is working in Human Resources, raising a teenage daughter, shelling for sand dollars, and surfing. She lives in New Jersey with her husband, daughter, and two dogs.